the dream and
the reality of
moving to colorado
told as pure fantasy

by terry ulick

boilerplate

colorado dreamin'

acknowledgments

Special thanks to Rachael who welcomed a wayward author with an open heart and kind understanding.

To Mick, on his quest and for sharing his vision in the photographs featured in this book. A great photographer, wonderful spirit, and friend.

Finally, to Bethany. Someone who travelled to Colorado where she found a dream realized. She also graces the covers of this book, proving pictures speak more than a thousand words.

introduction

The bright lights of Denver are shinin' like diamonds
Like ten thousand jewels in the sky
And it's nobody's business where you're goin'
Or where you come from
And you're judged by the look in your eye
  — Willie Nelson

This book has a long and fascinating history.

An eternity ago, back in 1972, I was teaching at a college outside of Chicago. My mother moved there to be with her new husband and I left Denver to be near her as she was terminally ill. It was the hippie era. All was changing or being reinvented. Mary, a dear friend from the college I taught at started an experiential education program. Filled with students not wanting establishment-dictated course doctrine pounded into them, they mirrored the changing times. Mary felt strongly life experience should be given college credit; a view not shared by the conservative educators running schools at the time. I couldn't help but love her. She was taking on the world!

She had gathered professors who were rag-tag hippie types perfect for the program. Like the students, they too hoped for change in the establishment education models.

Mary and I hung out when we weren't teaching or sitting in on encounter groups of first years students looking for alternative lifestyles or just listening to the Moody Blues. We both loved dropping in on her program's classes and watching her dream become a reality. Seeing a new world taking form, she'd smile at me, enjoying the wild classroom discussions as much as I did. Most memorable, we joined a class where the question posed to students by the biker professor dude was, "If you could live anywhere, where, and why?"

Great topic. He knew most all there wanted to get away from their childhood homes to live someplace where they could be free to sing and dance and love. Ah, good times, good times.

Sitting in a lecture room with tiered bench seating we cuddled together, happy to be there, only intending to listen in with me taking a few photographs to document the program. We looked at each other, both with eyes wide thinking it was an excellent and valuable question. Neither of us were from the Chicago and we both missed our native homes. Mine, Colorado, hers, Oklahoma. Striking a chord with all students there, hands raised in the air, all wishing to share their dream destination.

First up were two boys, each essentially saying, "Anywhere we can have girls stay over." That resulted in cheers from all there, Mary nudging me, whispering in my ear she was glad I had my own place. As we smiled at each other, I noticed one girl who sat with quiet assurance, her hand raised, patient in manner. In my eyes she was the poster child for how a hippie should look. Tall, skinny, gauze top from India, wonderfully snug faded bell-bottomed jeans, and her form was graced by long, brown hair parted down the middle with two strategically placed braids pulling her hair off her lovely face. Beads around wrists, neck and around her waist, slung low on an angle completed her ensemble.

Called after the first two boys, she rose slowly and gracefully from her first-row bench, turning around to see the entire class, telling everyone, no matter what the *man* said, "Move to Denver."

Nodding the "knowing" nod so typical of righteous hippies at the time, she explained how beautiful, open-minded, and groovy it was.

"Denver, man…
It's in the mountains…
Gentle people living in peace…
And, like, it's one big commune."

Then she told there was no pollution, people grew their own food, a place in the red rocks of mountains to listen to far-out music, the guys there were all burning their draft cards and pot was going to be legal.

Bike dude professor Jim stood, nodding as she proclaimed heaven on Earth, then looked up to me knowing it was where I was from. He smiled at Mary, wondering if it was okay to have me join the discussion. Mary nodded to him and nudged me, saying, "Raise your hand!" It was a tricky moment as I didn't wish to burst any bubbles or dash any dreams but saw no harm finding out more about what "Denver" was really like. I raised my hand. Jim explained I had moved from Colorado recently and asked if I could share my impression of the mile high city. I stood, and most all the students knew me and they were all looking at me. I looked at the girl, who was gently standing, appearing to glow, looking angelic, eyes up to me, waiting.

Having only recently left Colorado, I asked her when she was last there.

"It sounds great, and maybe it's because I lived high up in the Rockies, not down in Denver, it may have changed since then. When were you there last?"

With her dream-like quality, as if floating a few inches above the ground, she was a beautiful visage of the counterculture. She looked at me with such sincerity in her eyes. She said something I'll always remember.

"Well, I've never been there, but I heard John Denver sing about it."

Sitting back down after thanking the girl, Mary was smiling with delight. I couldn't help but smile too.

Mary later shared the girl's starry-eyed perception was what her new program was about. The dream of a better place and a better life. A class setting that welcomed dreams and ideals. A place to share experiences. Life experiences rather than notions gleamed from pop stars, media or movies. We agreed facing truth had its place, but dreaming came first. It would always be essential.

It was at that moment, looking at the girl, I realized it was more than a dream or fantasy when she spoke of Denver. It was a place she needed to find. Where she longed to be. This book is about the dream, and need, people have of Denver when planning to move here.

Popular music, TV and movies have a way of creating expectations of lifestyles, relationships, and places. Denver and all of Colorado are places media has glamorized and loves portraying as a unique place. Is it filled with people from UFOs like Robin Williams in Mork & Mindy? Is it the brooding, haunting Stanley Kubrick version of Stephen King's Overlook Hotel with Jack Torrance roaming in the maze? Is it the old west and log cabins and fishing for trout? Is it endless outdoor activities all the time, everyday? Is it what media tells us? A fantasy?

I only know each person moving to Colorado or Denver is experiencing is a voyage of discovery. I think about how that girl hearing a John Denver album about life in the Rockies was heard by many people, and many of them eventually moved here. I have often thought of what they expected, then what they found once here.

The dream. Then a realization. That is what each person moving to Colorado has once here.

Me, I'm still looking for the John Denver version complete with that beautiful hippie girl guiding me there. Up around the bend.

Oops.

That's CCR and Louisiana. Another college, another girl.

Okay, I just checked my antique vinyl collection. Yep. CCR. Credence Clearwater Revival. Yep, another college, another girl.

Another dream.

Terry Ulick
Writing from the high Rockies of Colorado
A place of dreams
A place I call home

stories

almost heaven

science fiction

Having grown up listening to the songs of John Denver touting all the wonders of Colorado, there was one song that started me writing fiction about the fantasy of being in, or living, in Colorado. The song, Take Me Home (Country Roads) *remains popular worldwide. The most amazing thing is that he didn't write it, and it isn't about Colorado.*

Perhaps just the name "Denver" on the recording made people think it was about Colorado. At heart it is about going home. What a wonderful notion. Going home. Going back to the place you belong. Even for those not from Colorado, their longing for a place that combines a decent life with the majestic beauty of the Rockies is a call to a place they know should be their home. John Denver wasn't originally from Colorado and he was wise to use the name "Denver" for his stage name. It was the right time to connect with the longing in America for a place of beauty and wonder.

His father was a pilot, and he was too. Colorado is home to aerospace industry. It's home to Air Force academies, and for a short time, the Space Force Academy.

This story combines the longing for home with graduates from the Space Force Academy far from their home in the mountains far away.

Looking at her out the port window rather than viewing her on a screen, he always marveled watching Anne.

Thinking back to the first time he saw her in a flight suit, at first he wasn't sure she was even in the huge thing. Seeing the large, bulky EVA relic used long ago on early missions, it was certainly moving. Having her name tag on it he guessed she had to be inside of it somewhere.

He stood evaluating her attempt as a first timer navigating various obstacles with care. He was tasked with finding a cadet for his next mission and as flight commander he preferred choosing promising new academy graduates himself. Heading up the longest voyage and space mission to-date, his crew were all veterans of deep space missions. Any new crew member needed to be exceptional. He continued watching Anne who wore the centuries-old suit intended to be the final physical challenge. It was an important test for any cadet as it had too much insulation, too much tank, and too heavy to walk around in as it was designed for the weightlessness of space, not Earth gravity.

Smiling as he remembered her on that day, he could see her trudging to the mock craft in the large hanger, looking up the ladder to the landing grid, climbing it, then somehow making it through the hatch. Tested in full gravity, getting into the simulator was a newbie's final test.

Anne was one of many names on a long list that day. Succeeding her climb into the mock craft, she became a crew member, no longer a newbie with her face covered by the vintage gold visor. Tapping her name on his tablet, he used his intuition and gave her crew status. She'd work directly with him. Looking at her name on the crew list, not quite understanding why, she intrigued him. Thinking first it was only because she made it to the hatch wearing the ancient suit without complaining, that wasn't why. Gazing at her, he realized it was the "e" at the end at her name. Anne, with an "e." He thought to call her Annie, and maybe that could be her crew moniker. He smiled, realizing she wasn't just Ann.

She was Anne, with a letter at the end never pronounced when saying her name. There was more about her to discover.

Hoping she would be capable of talking after the exertion of the test, she was busy getting out of the suit as he went to meet and congratulate her.

Looking at her in the simulator staging area, he was amazed how small she was. Wondering how she managed to move around in a suit heavy as her body, he was impressed. Studying her as he approached, he was taken with her simple beauty. She was small, had short pixie-cut hair and looked much like a little nymph in a book of fairy tales he cherished when he was a young child. She looked at him with dark brown eyes, blinking, looking fresh and confident. Remembering himself panting and exhausted when he was first tested in the suit, she showed no such fatigue. Smiling, then giving him a wink, she was fully out of the suit, letting it fall to the ground. Looking at it, then him, she shook her head.

"Silly thing..."

Lifting it up, heavy as it was, she managed to hang it on a hook. She turned back to face him. He asked if she meant the suit, or him?

Smiling, yet seeming mystified, she looked warmly into his eyes, asking, "Can't it be both?"

He was deep in the memory, then forced himself back to the present. Their craft was suspended in deep space, and so was Anne. Floating outside the port window, she was a sight to behold. Never again wearing the ancient suit he first saw her in, she wore the latest issue. Sleek and light as second skin, conforming to her, it accentuated her graceful form. Her movements were a mythical ballet. Free from gravity, suspended in the heavens, she swam in space, filling the emptiness with beauty. Nothing he had ever seen matched the freedom and joy of her untethered walks. He longed to be out there with her. Her partner in the dance.

Being the only two left alive on board the lonesome craft, he needed to remain in the ship. Knowing how much she loved the walks, he was content to stay inside while she danced in the starlight.

Seeing her returning, as on the first day they met, he went to greet her in the staging area. It was no simulation. This was what they trained for — surviving the horrors of events unexpected. Waiting for her to take off the suit, now with the generated gravity in the ship, she smiled at him as she let it fall, bent to lift it, then finished by hanging it on its hook. She ran to him, kissing him as they hugged.

"Next time, your turn. Okay?"

He would rather watch her enjoy herself. Shaking his head, he told her he was happy being with her, and that's all that mattered. He wanted her to have the walks the rest of the way. She hugged him tighter.

"John… Let's do one more… Together. There's no protocol not to. It doesn't matter now."

"I know, Anne. Look, we've made it this far… All the horrors… This ship doesn't have a crew anymore. It isn't in good shape. Not good to push our luck."

Looking at him and nodding, he felt her sadness. He could suit up and walk with her, but he didn't want to take any risks. They alone survived when all others hadn't. They had been given a chance. He doubted there would be another one. She knew he wanted to be with her. Both learned anything could happen. Both knew it already had. Looking up at him, she managed to smile again.

"We'll walk together whenever we feel like it once we're down. Funny, much as I love it out there, getting home, walking with the sunshine on my shoulders with you is all I really want."

Going to the galley for dinner, Anne selected music to go with their meal from her favorite playlist. She loved changing the song order to match their mood. He smiled at her as each song started. She smiled back, singing along. Playing ancient songs, he knew she was waiting for her favorite. Just before they finished eating, she lit up, telling him to get ready.

Country roads, take me home, to the place, I belong...

Laughing as he always did when she shouted out the chorus as the song played, he gently reminded her she wasn't from West Virginia, she was from Ohio. She pointed to the panel with picture of the man wearing funny glasses on the album cover.

"But his name is *Denver!*"

Laughing more, he reminded her she wasn't from Denver. He really just wanted to hear her say, as she always did, "That's where I met you. It's where you're from! It's why the crew called you *Denver...*"

I hear her voice, in the morning hour she calls me, the radio reminds me of my home far away...

He didn't understand how it could be possible, but he loved her more than ever. He nodded.

"I know."

And driving down the road I get a feeling that I should have been home yesterday, yesterday…

Letting the song finish, both knowing it wouldn't have been good to be home yesterday, they sat staring sadly at each other. Anne started crying, and looking at her filled him with emotion.

Jumping up, she sat on his lap, arms around his neck, crying as she hugged him with all her might. Holding her, feeling her shaking, he was forever lost in her. The only space that mattered to him now was deep inside of her. She was so small, so delicate, yet the most endless universe he could imagine. She filled up his senses like the mountain in springtime he hiked endlessly when growing up, looking for something, never knowing what until the day he saw her the first time.

Far from that day at the Space Force Academy where they met, they were alone in the void left by the madness consuming all others. Far from Earth, the final war began, and ended, in a mere day. Hearing the accounts and watching the video feeds, their ship's crew took sides, became enraged, savagely fighting to the death over the same conflicts that destroyed civilization on Earth. They hadn't joined in the crew's hidden hatreds. When the news was heard, the crew growing incensed, grabbing their suits they went for a tethered spacewalk waiting outside the ship until the crew gained their senses. Staring at the fighting inside the ship through the video image in their visors, that didn't happen. The ship's radios went quiet as there was no one inside the ship left alive. A bright flash from the portals meant someone hit the full decontamination device. Destroying any organisms on board, without suits on the crew was dust on the floor when they made it through the hatch as they both had trained to do so well.

That was their last space walk together. Months passed, and they had nothing except each other and their home far away.

Anne was as determined as the day she trudged in the heavy suit to put hope in John's heart. Stopping the ship, turning it around, she calculated they had enough power to make it back to Earth with the ship navigating the route. She knew what waited. Neither were expecting to find anything or anyone left. She wasn't looking for the past. That was gone.

Approaching the blue sphere, once home to billions, they held hands while staring at Earth's beauty through the portal. Blue waters and white clouds rotated beneath the ship. It didn't take long to see their destination. Anne jumped with excitement as they saw the thin line of the Mississippi, the green plains to its west, then the rise of mountains. Nodding to her, he found himself smiling despite of the obvious.

"Anne. That's a whole new world down there. It will be a place we've never known before. Like the Garden. Just us two. Are you ready? We don't know what Denver will be like."

Looking at him, she said the first words she ever spoke to him, knowing he would understand.

"Silly thing…"

She took his hand, leading him to the landing craft. She winked at him as they put on their suits.

"It will be just like the song says. *Almost Heaven.*"

the denver job interview

humor

This story was inspired by the great straight-faced master of the only-hear-one-side-of-a-conversation comedian, Bob Newhart.

Many people know him as the Buddy's dad in the Christmas movie, Elf. *Watching the movie recently, I thought back to his wonderful stand-up routines where he would pretend to be speak to someone on the phone, hearing only his side of the conversation. His reactions to what was being said on the other end of the call was hilarious.*

I found myself thinking of him working at a progressive company as the HR manager, interviewing a job candidate. Just the thought of him in Colorado was funny but having him do a job interview with someone new to the area was a great inspiration for this story.

All that is needed is to picture Bob Newhart (or person of your choice) on one side of a desk, conducting a job interview with someone new to Colorado and not sure if the candidate will fit into the corporate culture.

 .

Donald, hey, please, sit, make yourself comfortable. I'm glad you were able to come in on short notice, especially in this weather. When it's this cold, snow makes roads pretty slick. Much traffic? None? Really? Well, I guess that's normal when it's like this. I bet it was just you and a bunch of snowplows lined-up side-by-side. It was? Well, then I'm glad you left early. Very impressive with this blizzard. You made it on time. Glad you came in. I'm excited.

What? Oh, yes. They weren't doing that on purpose. The plow trucks drive like that… in formation. Must be a reason. How'd your 4-wheeler do in this snow? Oh, you don't have one? No, I'm not familiar with that one. You have a Spark. Really? Spark… Spark. Isn't that some new SUV? No? Small car? Tiny. Good gas mileage and all? That's a good reason right there. You know, I thought they stopped making cars. Wow, I haven't seen a car in a long time. Not many SUVs now either. Everyone loves their pickups. I just had mine jacked up. 40-inch tires, two-foot lift, winch, even ten-inch spike wheel bolts. That beast can handle anything. Oh, thank you for the compliment. Saw it in the garage? Yep, well, yeah… a little hard to get around it with the brush guard and extended cab and hitch. But, a great rig. Perfect ride if I ever get up past the foothills. Lots of snow up there, I hear.

No, no. I don't live up there. Ya know, I actually don't know anybody who lives up the mountains. Me? I live just about a mile down the street from here. First street plowed. Short ride. We do go up to Conifer every Thanksgiving to cut our own Christmas tree. But heck, we rent a Suburban for that. Trees can really mess up the paint with the sap. Spares my candy-flake finish. Kids love it. Well, when you finish moving here I'll hook you up with my dealer. I suggest a pickup, not any of those SUVs, though. Anyway, first things first. Business… Oh, I forgot. I know a place you can cut a tree and they'll load it on top for you. Remember to get the directions from me. Okay. Business. So, yes, I've studied your resume, and I just love it. The job stuff is great, all there. Super, super. Yep. But, just some tedious blanks to fill in. Sound good? Ready? Oh, yes. You missed some on the job app.

Let's see. No… Not many missing. Some. It happens. So many questions. Easy to fix as you're here. So, yes. Education, super. Impressive. Interned at the right places. Good. References from friends of the owner. Well, can't beat that! I see your dad gave him the cash to start this company.

Well, I bet he's happy he did. Our IPO made a lot of people very happy. Job history… well, just out of school with your shiny new PhD, so we can plug your intern stints in for that. Super. The job qualifications fit the requirements nicely, so no more to do there. Now, you did fill in your personal goal. A bit long… Think you could sum it up in a sentence or two? I'll type it in. Best to make it brief. How would you sum it all up? Let's see… Yep, you used all 100 characters. Yep, that box. The one where you're free to sum it all up.

Not enough room? Really? We just expanded it, but now it's so much to read and people are very busy. Let's see… I think we can get it down to a sentence. It asks where do you want to be in five years? I've got my fingers on the keys, ready to fly! Don't wear 'em out!

Okay. Sure… Yes. You certainly do know what you want. So, you want to say… five years from now…

"Learned the business, contributed to the success of the company, obtained management position?"

That about right?

I'm putting all of that in. Ahhh… May still be too long. Typing. Typing. Typing. Oops. Ran out of space. Still too long. What can we cut?"

Okay, let's try it that way… Learned the business, obtained management position. Yep, it fits. Buttt… I don't know if that really is better.

Hmm. Let me think. What? Well, yes, I have. I've seen what gets people hired. Here's what I think will impress everyone. This is neat! Your objective in five years is… okay, hold on. Yes.

"Working."

Hmm? That's right. One word says it all. Working! In five years you want to be working. Yes, that will do it. Certainly. That will impress people here. What?

Do you know how many people come here and don't have a job in five years? A lot. I tell you, it's not that we let them go. They're off to those parks, hanging with friends. They are so busy because we have so many things to do here. We understand work isn't always the number one priority. But you? Working! This will be very impressive. So, sound good? It says it all, okay? Change it someday? Sure. This is just for right now. Okay, moving on...

Okay, the next things were all blank The boxes not checked. Hmm? No, all incomplete. Maybe the form skipped past these. No worry. I'll just read them off, you tell me if I should check the box. Which ones? Oh. The ones all about your personal interests, hobbies, things like that. Ready? Okay, good. Tell me if you are interested in, have done, or doing any of the following.

Skiing?

Naw. Really? Don't ski? Okay, no snow where you're from, so that could be why. Interested in skiing?

Nope. Never thought about it? So, a No. Sure? Okay. Typing away here. Not now. Maybe someday. Why put that? Well, skiing is really big here, but there's a lot more.

So, Hiking?

Really? Happy with your treadmill? So, kind of like hiking. Not on the list though. So. No to hiking. There are a ton of great trails all around here. Hey, don't those treadmills have a screen where it shows going down a path? Do they have ones of Colorado trails? If they did, I could put those down. No? Yours doesn't have a screen? Well, worth asking. Alright, I'll leave that one blank.

Biking?

That is something I would not have guessed. Afraid of biking. Hit by a big pickup truck when riding your bike when just a kid? Haven't been on one since? Oh, that's not good. We may be able to help with that. Provide therapy. What? Don't you want to overcome that fear if we paid for counseling, even? Ohh, you're in therapy… oh, still… Have been since it happened… That must have been some accident. Sorry about that.

Okay, now this one, no skiing down hills and running into a hiker or bike.

Camping?

Tricky for you? I understand. You have allergies and tried it when you were younger? Ouch! Your face swelled up and throat closed up? Doc said a tent isn't best with allergies? You have to be careful then. Sure. Of course. A question, well, just to fill in the picture. Was that camping trip before, or after, the bike thing?

Same vacation?

Okey-dokey, makes sense. Sure does. Family outings can be like that. Well, let's keep going. But, I kinda think this may be something you probably did on that same trip. Three things, all kind of similar.

Canoeing? Rafting? Kayaking?

You did? I thought that might be the case. Ohh, ohh, no! Oh... Hurts to think about that one, and it didn't even happen to me. Oh, that's awful. That really happened to you? I thought it may be something from that trip, but that is just plain scary.

Look, I'll just run down the rest. No need to relive that vacation, alright? Good. Anything hits, shout out a yes. Okay?

Zip lines? Didn't think that had a chance.

Oh, my God... Climbing? Yes. Like that kind. Yes, scaling those mountains out the window. Climbing those. Big "No" to that one.

Cross country skiing? Just you, on flat land. Soft, fluffy snow... Okay, no. That probably answers the snow shoe question. Yeah.

Hunting? Alright. Now, remember... You do have the advantage there. Lots of elk and things. You're the one with the rifle. Oh, vegetarian, I understand.

Ballooning? Gentle, get to see the Rockies from above, peaceful and quiet. Fraid it will crash? Don't hear much about that, but, a No to that.

Here's one that isn't risky, and man, it is so popular.

Golf?

Really. Man, that is rough. Really! Your ex-girlfriend was semi-pro? Dumped you for a pro? Why you wanted to move and come here? No, oh, I agree. That can really hurt. "No" to golf with an exclamation mark…

Getting to the end of the outdoors stuff near Denver. Last one of them is spelunking. Oh, fancy term for cave exploring. Relics, dinosaur bones, gold… So, you're claustrophobic? Who could have guessed? Well, big plus for continuity, though.

Ready for some general interests? May be a bit better for you. What? Don't worry one bit. All those we just went through, well, all it really shows is you're not much of an outdoors type. So, ready?

These are all fun things. Here goes.

Well, we have Concerts at Red Rocks. Great outdoor venue for music. Really? Afraid of crowds? Kind of goes along with being claustrophobic I bet. Yeah? I thought so.

Okay, next, Sports Events. Broncos. Big NFL team. College ball at U of C, in Boulder. Oh, I see. Same problem. Let's move on.

Photography. All the mountains and wildlife, great to take pictures of. Ohh. Yeah. I see. That is true. You'd have to hike, bike, climb and maybe even camp to get those types of pictures. Ah, that's too bad. I hoped that would be a Yes.

Volunteering? Really? Yes? Alright! Really? All through school, too? Oh, yes. There's a spot for what you volunteer for… okay… That's really something… Hmm. That sure shows you're doing your part… but, maybe let's leave it blank for now as that's not a Denver activity. I agree. Well, that's progress. Now, this one surprises even me, but lots of people are into it.

Brewing Beer. Yep, all the zillions of microbreweries around Denver and Boulder. Oh, yes, there are lots of those here. They started out from kitchens and basements. Alright, water only, don't drink. Now, this one, well, I think they put it in just for fun.

Miniature golf?

Ohh. Not that either! Ahh, bummer. Reminds you of her? Ahh, no, really, don't tell me that. Perfect form? No handicap? On televised tour right now? Absolutely. If you turn on the local news she may be headlining the sports? Line of clubs, big endorsements? I feel for you on that one. Ouch!

Okay, there is a spot here where you can fill in other interests or hobbies. Oh, I see your eyes light up. Okay! Tell me about your… da da de daaa! Other interests or hobbies! C'mon, lay it on me.

So, I'll just put that in, yep, right here. International traveling. Oh, I sure see the connection. The volunteering to do hunger relief in third world nations and rescue endangered species. That explains it. So, traveling and getting away from Denver is your main interest.

Well, while heading out to who knows where, remember you can take the secret underground UFO conspiracy theory tour of the airport at least. Oh, already done that? Enjoy it? Oh, yeah. Claustrophobic. Too close, too many people? Really? You had to run away but couldn't find the secret entrance or exit? Swat team called from the panic that caused? It went that far? No, no. Sure. Panic attacks like that make people say some scary stuff. Oh, that was nice. No charges. I understand. So, the bike therapy got put on hold to help you deal with being trapped in the basement at DIA and all that news coverage? Woah! I hope you didn't watch through to the sports segment... Oh, good. Doubled your therapy sessions? I hope that works out.

What? The importance of these questions? Well, yes. A little bit of a concern... No, please, don't look like you're at DIA about to get tased again. It's cool. Ah, well, it's because most people move to Denver and look for a job here because of the...

I know, I know. Thanks for pointing that out. Silly for me to start repeating the list. After this you'll sure remember the whole list of what brings people here. It is a big reason. Everyone loves it here because of the hiking, biking, camping, rafting, climbing, skiing, music... Oh! I'm sorry. Hey, just call me Brittany cause, oops, I did it again! I know. I think it's all good. You've explained why those are all things you really can't do at all. What? Well, yes, they matter to some extent. Those interests are considered when hiring. We like finding staff that fits our, secret on this one, very pricey location. All those attractions help us get top talent from around the world. Hmm? I know, yes, you certainly do, you travel internationally. No, you're right. Those are not job skills, but... somewhat important part of the culture here. Yes, hmm? You certainly have the job skills and I know you would be a great addition to the team when it comes to the work. What? I have a "look?" Really. What kind of look?

I did not realize I was doing that. Sorry, I didn't mean to have a funny expression. That is not right. When I said "team," correct? Yes. I do think that will be a question raised. Well, let me explain. This company is really,

really big on team building. Corporate retreats. Love corporate outings too. Learning to rely on each other. Build trust. Share values. And, interests. If you look at our site, go leadership, interests, Yeah. That page. Can you see it on your phone? Yes, see everyone says hiking biking skiing climbing and all the rest in their bio? Company values. What? No, they each wrote their own. Sounds like a template? Naw. Back to the team thing? Okay?

Teams here are built by all the managers going out to some beautiful place, like, well, Rocky Mountain State Park. Or, sometimes, some ski resort. Usually for about a week. Sometimes they rent a remote cabin. Or, even in the cold, camp out. I can tell you from experience you really learn who is there for you when you're repelling a straight cliff. You know, I think you're the first person I've interviewed who doesn't check off all those interests, so something new. Haven't had that before. Well, yes. It may be a challenge for staff here. You know how it is. Standing in the halls, talking at lunch. Those are the things people talk about. They have those in common. But, not my place to determine the fit.

Well, your application is all done. I'll pass it on up to the top. What? Not at all. I assure you, your skills are super and I'm sure those can be important too. I'll get in touch when the top team gets back next week.

Yes, I'm sure that's what they're out doing. Thank you for going through the list, very brave. Oh, know it by heart now?

I think you're super smart and, hey, on work skills, you can probably do the job better than most with all the time you have as you're not out doing the other stuff! Okay, I'll share that you have your reasons, and I guarantee the top team will look at your application. Yes, as I said, well, the top team is away. Oh, no need to tell me. I know they're all out doing… Oh! Let's end it here. Please. You don't want to hear what they're out doing. I think you understand, though.

Got everything? Good. Now, please be careful heading back. All that snow is great for sk… ahh, snow… snow… yes! It's great for the snow cap and water supply. Yeah. But not so hot driving a little car. What was the name of yours again? Why?

Oh, crazy thing. I don't know how it started. People somehow get handles, you know, nicknames, usually the same as their car. The CEO is Nav, for his Navigator. Oh, me? Well, they call me Silver. Not for my gray hair, my Silverado. So maybe we'll have a Sparky on board soon.

No, not a snowboard!

how to find denver

urban fantasy

There is a strange behavior when someone moves to a place they learn is special. Somehow thinking they were let in on a great secret, they quickly start worrying that "everybody" is going to move there and ruin it!

Soon, they start noticing out-of-state license plates, muttering obscenities from those horn-in opportunists from California or Texas or Wisconsin. It doesn't matter where they are from, they don't belong here! Go back! Go home! This is my place!

Most likely they still have their California or New Jersey license plates, making it even sillier. People learn to quickly get the green and white mountain landscape Colorado plates to not be cut off on the freeway or get a ding in their door at a Kings Sooper.

This story came from creating a Spotify playlist to listen to while writing these stories.

I experienced what is told in this tale of seeking true love, a nice place to live, and listening to songs written about Colorado. It's a fact that Colorado inspires great songs, and has more than most other cities. This is how one new transplant found Denver through a playlist about many different places to live.

"A relationship based on needs is destined to fail. Once the need is filled, there must be more there to want."

by terry ulick

That was advice a good friend gave when I was starting out in life. Understanding it was in reference to relationships, it made perfect sense. If you fall in love with someone because they like to party, once you're home and the party's over, what then? Talk about the party?

That advice also proved valuable as I faced other types of life changes. Following that wisdom, I started thinking about my future, not alone, but in a relationship based on shared values and interests — not a life based only on needs. The future I longed for would be about what I really wanted. Finding a love, and friends, who liked similar movies, music, cars, places to go, authors, even fast-food places. The list was an important one and it served me well in thinking about what was most important as I looked ahead.

As time went on, I began to realize the same principal applied to just about everything. I thought about work. You need a paycheck, but if you don't like what you're tasked with, people you work with, the hours or the workplace, those begin to be issues larger than the paycheck you *need*. Those are things you *want* in a job. Once the money's in the bank, you still have to go to work.

Stuck in a rut, I was excited about making a change. First, I decided it was time to move. That was clearly both want *and* a need. A new start. Part of settling down and meeting someone to have a serious relationship with had me wanting to buy my first house.

All of the planets had aligned, and I was ready to make a major change as I entered my thirties. I'd partied enough. Most of my friends wanted to continue partying but that was no longer the life I wanted. All of that combined with news from the company I work for letting me know I could work remotely from home permanently. That meant I could move

colorado dreamin'

anywhere and I started thinking of a place where I could afford a house of my own. With all that in mind, it just became a matter of where best to move. It had to be affordable, fun, and a city large enough to have plenty of people to meet, nice things to do with new friends, and if all went well, a love to share it all with me.

Going to clubs, hanging out; all that seemed pointless to me and I realized it had gotten old and wasn't what I wanted. Now farther along in life, I was thinking more of meeting people who went to museums, sporting events, concerts, volunteering, and into outdoor activities. I was proud of my list beyond my need to move someplace new. After the move, it had to be more than just a place to sleep and eat. Living someplace is a relationship, a big one, and the place had to be filled with all the interesting things I wanted to do.

One thing I like about streaming music services, especially my favorite, Spotify, is how easy it is to search and find all types of songs. I'm not sure how the idea came to me but I began making playlists about cities; about living someplace so special people wrote songs about it. Looking back, I think it may have been a Spotify recommended playlist of old boomer tunes that came up because I listened to some Elton John song that had to have been at least fifty years old.

The playlist was *"60s & 70s Hits"* — all singer/songwriter stuff. No current tunes, but easy enough to listen to while driving. Two songs caught my attention because they were about going someplace to live, or maybe just visit. The first was a total folk thing telling people to go to San Francisco and wear flowers in their hair. Well, I was sharing a one-bedroom in San Francisco with four others and paying over two grand a month for a beanbag on the floor, so, nope! No flowers in my hair. I couldn't afford a flower or much of anything else, and it was the place I needed to get away from.

The next song was one of those begging and pleading songs. *Baby please stay, baby don't leave me.* I guess it was because the guy sang, "*Please come to Boston in the springtime.*" Maybe they had remote work from home relationships back then. I got the point. I hadn't realized it, but apparently there were tons of songs about places to move to and how wonderful they were.

Enlightened by the playlist, it turned out that geezers loved to write and sing about moving to special places, so I started doing searches on Spotify using names of cities. I figured if there were a lot of songs about a place, that would help me find the lifestyle I wanted. Looking at the artists, it seemed all the singers were the types who loved going to museums and music events, riding electric scooters and playing at outdoor gigs. It was worth a try.

To test my theory, I searched for Des Moines. A few local choirs and marching bands (having the city in their band name), showed up but nothing about the joy of moving there. Made sense. So, to see one that had to of inspired a lot of songs, I searched for New York. That validated my idea. All kinds of songs about New York showed up, and from a wide range of artists — although most of them were ones I didn't know. There we're plenty of songs about the city. Tons. The top one was "*New York New York,*" by a dead guy named Sinatra. I listened to it and the lyrics were pretty good.

Start spreading the news
I'm leavin' today
I'll make a brand new start of it
In old New York

Then, what really grabbed me was when he sang,

colorado dreamin'

If I can make it there
I'll make it anywhere

Interesting. So, move there, get so beat up by prices and all that crime stuff that after living there you could survive just about anyplace better than there! Inside track, for sure. Thanks, crooner guy! I scratched NYC off my list.

There were more New York songs, but most were other people singing the same song different ways. There were lots of odes to *falling in love again* in New York, *falling in love with New York* again, then quite a few going on and on about some big park and shopping at Christmas-time there, but none really about moving there. Most were about getting out of the place.

Searching on Chicago was helpful. Lots of different songs. Lyrics calling it that "*toddlin' town, that won't let you down.*" But that was by that same Sinatra guy so he must have got around. There was a band named Chicago. Songs about the Chicago Cubs. "*Go, Cubs, Go!*" Not too many "gotta leave" Chicago songs, but not much about why to move there.

I tried a lot of other city names, and Los Angeles had a several songs about moving there. Most by some group who apparently were really into conservation as they named themselves The Eagles. It turned out after viewing the lyrics as the songs played, they were pretty ominous and scary. Dark desert highways, witchy women, desperadoes. After those, a bunch from all kinds of singers about it being for star-struck actors and performers and how they got used up and spit out. Yuck! I'm glad I searched that place. Yikes!

Using WeatherBug to view a map of both climate and the whole country, I realized I had overlooked Denver. Typing it into the search, home run.

Go, Rockies, Go! Endless songs about Denver. And, lots about Colorado too. Not all the same song or the same artists either. Just from the song names, I realized Denver was a goldmine. Just about each song had a title or messages saying, "*I Need to Go to Denver, I Want to Go to Denver, My Love Waits in Denver.*" Lots of the same sentiments and phrases for Colorado and the Rocky Mountains too. One said it perfectly.

Goin' out to Denver
See what I can find
Goin' out to Denver
See what I can find
Maybe find somebody
Be a good friend of mine

No toddlin' town, or spreadin' the news, or checking in but never checking out stuff. At last!

The playlist was too long to listen to all the songs, but after a couple of hundred, I was pretty convinced both Denver and Colorado had won the hearts of decent, sensitive types most likely to have "wants-based" relationships. They didn't "need" to go to Denver, they wanted to. That's a big difference. I speak from experience. My past relationships were based on a need — for a night or two but, hey, I was young and foolish. That wasn't want I wanted now. Well, not that I wasn't looking for a rockinhot love, but one who was all sensitive and caring, like me now. I wanted to find someone who liked mountains and real eagles — not some stoned-out hippies flying high or driving in some fast lane.

The Denver songs were about finding someone out on a mountain hike, shacking up in some cabin on a stream, watching the sunset or sunrise or both if you had reached that point in a committed relationship, plus endless live recordings where the singer talked about how beautiful the stars were and they could be seen when they performed at some red rock place. I couldn't figure that out because none of them played rock, just acoustic coffee house stuff.

If every singer ever holding a guitar loved Denver, then it was a good bet I would too. I Googled it, and yep, all the stuff they sang about showed up as organic listings. Endless natural wonders. National parks. Mountains nearby. Universities. Wildlife. The house and rents weren't as low as I hoped, but better then San Francisco. I was running on a Bay Area paycheck, so hey, I could outbid anybody. It looked good to me. Places to eat, famous schools, and enough people there to find ones who came for the same reasons as me. Spotify subscribers from everywhere but Denver, all of them just like me so we'd have that in common right from the start.

It was easy to offer a hundred over asking price for a house with three actual bedrooms — and "mountain view." For a moment I thought I goofed up and had found a home next to Redwood City or Palo Alto. Mountain View? Oh, a real mountain, not some fifties sub-development shack that got lucky on tech dollars.

After buying a Jeep Wrangler because every picture of people in Colorado I saw had them driving one, I packed my beanbag and grabbed my backpack then crossed the bridge to get on 80, heading for the city a mile above sea level, then just past the Rockies. Before I left I made a playlist about leaving the Bay Area. Just one song. Seemed fitting. Some old-timer of a crooner singing, "*I left my heart in San Francisco.*" I liked it, but thought it needed to be updated. It really should be he left his flowers there. Oh, his money too!

Overall, my playlist was a great way to get the lowdown on the lodo

(Denver speak for lower downtown where all the hot clubs and bars are). No bridge tolls, fun things — all close by. I complain to new friends the only thing I could do without is all the people moving here from California. I know my new friends didn't because they let you know with their "NATIVE" sticker on their cars. I was looking at one of those stickers at a gas station to see what they cost. The guy behind the counter, seeing me looking at the sticker, asked me if I had just moved here from California. That reminded me I really needed to register my Jeep and get rid of those California plates. That, and get it all muddy like the ones without the Native stickers.

Now all I need to do is take some ski lessons, find any *In and Out* burger locations here, and buy a second beanbag for when I meet that good friend of mine.

Settled down with my new furry friends, a dog and cat, and my *Home Repair For New Homeowners* book, I can finally stop listening to my city songs playlists. I didn't *want* or *need* to move to Denver anymore. I had *moved* there. Now I'm singing a new song and have a whole new playlist.

colorado love affair

romance

I know many people who've moved to Colorado. Denver in most instances because their true love had a job offer or their job was moved here.

Following your love to Denver is common, and a good reason to move as there are new jobs and opportunities as the city grows faster than most others.

Sometimes the move survives a relationship that doesn't survive. People change or grow apart and they decide to stay in the mile-high city and make a new life for themselves. I know of one such story, and it's one where I can't drive down most streets in Denver without being reminded of how strange moving for love can be.

Driving to the just-opened burger joint, I looked at the police directing traffic, making a lane for the mile-long line of cars waiting to get a fresh-made burger and fries — and bragging rights that they had eaten lunch at the trendiest place to be seen in Denver even though it was dinner by the time they reached the drive-through window. I wasn't interested in the food served, the oh-so-urban staff, the long wait, or being on top of trends. I didn't get in the long line of determined drivers willing to wait all day for a hamburger and fries. I was only there to take a picture of the line of cars and send it to a friend who had asked me how Peter was faring in Colorado.

Thirty years ago I met the love of my life while she was on vacation in Colorado where I lived. She was from California, and I kept my home but moved to be with her. It was a tough call, but I knew we would move to Colorado one day as my home was waiting once her parents retired as they planned to move to where it was less expensive and travel. It worked out well as I started a fast-food burger chain in California. It grew from one drive-through stand to nearly 500 locations in 26 states all serving fresh meat smashed onto a grill. No frozen patties or fries. The time was right for good food served fast, and I went from smashing burgers and flipping them to running a large enterprise where I spent my time looking for managers and new locations. I eventually sold the business to an investment group and needed to find someone to take over my job managing the chain as I planned to retire young with my fresh burger cash and for my wife and I to move home to Colorado.

That's when I hired Peter. He was young, married, smart, ambitious and I thought him a good choice to take over my role and keep the success of the chain growing. Teaching him all I could about running the operation, he learned fast and I knew he was going to continue on and make the business even more successful than I had.

One thing about running a successful chain of burger places is that most of the staff is young and hoping to grow into management positions. One such staffer was Jeanie. She was one of my first managers, and I will admit I thought her a charmer and very attractive. She was a manager because she was ambitious and smart, making it clear she wanted to be part of the company's success. Jeanie was the type of person anyone running a growing business hoped to have on staff and she worked hard and deserved to rise through the ranks. Eventually, she moved from managing a stand to working at corporate headquarters scouting new locations.

Hiring Peter, I noticed that he connected with Jeanie and as she was experienced in store operations, I was glad they were working together as she had moved up through the ranks and could share her insights with my replacement.

Well, it turned out to be a bit more than that. Living not far from the main office where both Peter and Jeanie worked along with me, I passed by the headquarters coming home late one night, near midnight, and saw their cars in the lot and one office light on. Not thinking much more than they were working late after a location visit, I didn't give it any worry until a few days later when I was riding home after midnight and saw the same two cars and one office light on.

I can't say I started going out late to check the situation, but looking back I seem to remember being out late more often than usual and it concerned me as they were both married, and I hoped it was strictly business. It wasn't. I had learned Peter's marriage was having trials, and I knew Jeanie's husband from social events. He was in pharmaceutical sales and was on the road for long stretches. Putting it all together, I worried about all involved but what they did in their personal lives was none of my business unless it interfered with company operations.

It did.

Three months after noticing the late-night office activities, Jeanie came into my office one morning looking frazzled, nervous, and her face was flushed. Asking if she could close the door, I told her certainly, and that I was concerned as she looked upset. After sitting down, she asked if I could increase her salary. She had just gone through a performance review and had a substantial increase in pay. Pointing that out, I asked how much she had in mind.

"I've been talking to my husband, and he said since I'm working twice my normal hours since helping Peter, I should be making twice as much, so that's what I think I deserve. A doubling of my salary."

Remaining calm and mannered, I could only respond to the surprising request and not express my opinion that the extra hours had little to do with work.

"Jeanie, now that the company has new owners, I have must their increase policy. You just had a well-earned increase, so that's something done during an annual review. I don't think HR would consider that, and it may backfire if I asked. If your workload requires twice the hours, that isn't fair to you and I don't have to talk to HR for that answer. I'll create a new position to take that extra work on, letting you work regular hours again. So, no, I can't double your pay, and I'll post a new opening for an assistant so you will have a new person to help you. Does that sound fair? I'm sorry as I was not aware that your workload had increased so dramatically. Please, come see me if that should happen again."

She glared at me as she stood up, her face red with anger, walked out of the office, went to see Peter, then getting her coat walked out for the day. I didn't make an issue out of her leaving as she may have been going to a meeting or work-related event although I was certain she was just upset and was headed home.

Such incidents are upsetting, and I knew more would be coming with my refusal to pay for the late-night meetings. As the office filled up the next morning, Peter was in, but Jeanie was a no-show and hadn't called to say she was taking PTO or a sick day. I asked Peter to come to my office and inquired if Jeanie had called him. He was visibly upset, telling me she had, and she had given him a message for me.

"She won't be in today as she's livid that you won't pay her for all the hours she's here. She told me to tell you that she thinks you're a bastard, and frankly, I agree."

It was just the way he said it. It was so arrogant. How could he think I was so stupid and not know the hours were not about work as I would know if extra demands were placed on either of them. I found myself telling him I wished to talk outside of the office area, then led him to a janitorial closet and as I shut the door my adrenaline surged and I found myself saying, "I should flip you like a burger talking to me like that!"

I was hurt. I told him that I had been fair to both of them, offered to hire someone to help if extra hours were needed, and I knew about their working into the night, but also knew that no extra work was being done. He stared at me, realizing I wasn't falling for the situation they found themselves in, and he did stop the charade and said he understood, apologized and returned to his office.

Within the month, Jeanie gave notice. She had a job offer in Denver working for a new chain of gourmet burger eateries. After two weeks, she was gone. Once she left, Peter couldn't keep from looking depressed and sad. I invited him to lunch a week after Jeanie left and expressed my concern for him. He looked about to cry, and told me some sad news.

"My wife and I are getting a divorce. I'm a wreck, and I think it's unfair to be in the job you hired me for in this state. Also, and I think you can draw your own conclusion… I am thinking of starting over… moving to Denver."

Some people move for work, some for love. He was giving up a great job for love, and my heart went out to him as his whole life was turned upside down. Nodding, I told him it hurt to learn of his divorce and I would support whatever he chose. I assured him that if he needed references, I would give him high marks as he had been doing a great job.

After leaving the company, Peter moved to Denver. We kept in touch with a phone call every few months. I didn't ask, but he did mention that he hadn't seen much of Jeanie once there, and when he had seen her, she was arm-in-arm with the CEO of the new gourmet burger corporation. That was hard to hear. Divorcing his wife, moving to follow her, and then seeing her with her new boss was a sad story. He did say something that impressed me.

"You know, Denver is growing and there really aren't that many great burger joints like you made in California. I was thinking a place with simple, made-fresh burgers and fresh-cut fries is missing and would do good here. I'm thinking of opening a location and seeing how it goes."

Asking him if he needed any funding or help, he said he had his savings, and could get one off the ground.

"I learned from you. Start smart, start small, give value and quality, and don't have any investors."

That's how I did it, and I was glad to hear he learned that is a solid way to launch a business.

It took time, but the one thing Peter had that I liked was his sense of what was trending and missing in a market. He launched a burger chain that was the only one open all night. Soon the party crowd was lining up after the clubs closed, and they told all their friends, families and coworkers about the place. He filled a need for the after-party crowd that made his first burger stand the place to be seen. Soon, a second, then a third, and now near a hundred all over Colorado. He's one of the most successful in the field, and he's worth a fortune. He met a nice woman who he married, not a coworker, and they've been together for 20 years.

Moving back to Colorado, living in our mountain estate built with burger dollars from my own successful chain, I confess I have never eaten at one of his stands. I guess I have had enough burgers in my life, and somehow going to "Jeanie's Jive Burgers" just doesn't seem right.

Call me sentimental, but I think Jeanie helped him be the successful chain owner he is. On a call to him one time, I was straight and sincere when I told him he owed it all to her.

When my wife and I moved to Colorado, for me it was to go back home. For my wife it was for our love and all the stories I told her about how beautiful it was. Peter moved for love. Love can be fleeting, kind, or heartbreaking. But if you happen to move for love, Colorado is a good place to end up. Should the nature of relationships have you standing alone late one night out on Colfax Avenue wondering what you're going to do, have faith. Know there is at least one late-night burger joint to meet someone new. Chances are they're there for the same reason.

Peter understood having something to share is a nice way to start a relationship. If you're a vegan or can't handle gluten, I heard they have a meatless patty served on a bed of lettuce. Listen for someone ordering the gluten-free meatless monster and some fries. Even if you're a carnivore, order the same, say hello, and that you're new to Denver.

shining business opportunity

horror

It is amazing how popular the book and movie, The Shining by Stephen King, are with people all over the world. The story, set in Colorado, was inspired when the famous author and his wife found themselves in a beautiful hotel up in Estes Park at the gateway to Rocky Mountain State Park, but the only ones as they were there during a blizzard. Thinking how being the only ones in a grand hotel gave the writer inspiration for the best-selling novel, then movie, gave me inspiration for this tale.

People travel to Colorado just to stay in the famous room that inspired the novel. What they expect it will be, and what it turns out to be, can often be as surprising as the famous book or movie.

Jimmy grew up watching *The Shining*.

Although the movie scared him, he watched it whenever it was on cable TV. Then as he left home to be on his own he bought a DVD of it. Then a Bluray. And then a 4K disc.

Searching Amazon, he found an "Overlook" key fob for room 237 and used it on his keyring. Then, t shirts with the logo, then ones with Jack in his mad rage. And the rug pattern began being put on area rugs, shower curtains, window curtains, and prints in frames to hang on the wall above the rug and next to the window curtains. He bought all of them. He found a sticker, life-sized, of an ax cutting through a wood door, and he applied it to the inside of his bathroom door where he could see the broken and splintered wood flying as in the movie by pulling back the rug pattern shower curtain.

Along with the video discs he had the soundtrack on cassette, vinyl and CD. He found a book of the screenplay and put it next to his collection of hardcover and paperback editions of the Stephen King book, a collection that was growing larger as new editions with new covers and higher prices were released.

All that wasn't enough. Looking like a *Shining* Shrine, his apartment was full of memorabilia and collectible items, but any true fan of the book or movie knew that a trip to the hotel that inspired the story was a must. Doing extensive research, he found that many people had stayed in the room where Jack axed his way into the hearts of *Shining* fans worldwide and lived to tell about it. They all had stories of noises and hearing chopping, and some seeing the lumbering figure with an ax looking for Wendy, ready to sarcastically say, "Here's Johnny." He had his keyring, his t shirts, and he thought long about if he would be brave enough to spend the night in the room.

Wondering what the best time of the year was to go, he read that Stephen King and his wife were the only ones in the hotel one winter night, and had to stay because of a snow storm. He wanted to go the time of year when there was the best chance of a winter storm, and he would know the feeling of being trapped, of roaming halls looking for twins and valets and bartenders, and a wife and son he admittedly didn't have. It was then he came up with an idea that would make him a legend.

Although the hotel sold key rings, souvenirs, and rented the room out, without Wendy and little Danny the experience would not be complete. It was on the day when he decided to reserve the famous room he came up with the idea of hiring a Wendy and a Danny for anyone staying in room 237. For a brief moment he thought of using mannequins or even cardboard cutouts, but those were absurd gimmicks in his mind. He wouldn't be satisfied with such nonsense. No, he would need to find a tall, thin woman who looked just like Shelley Duvall, and a boy or two who looked like Danny. Add a blue gingham dress for Wendy, a vintage Big Wheel trike for Danny, and make sure they knew all the lines and could play the parts convincingly.

It was pure genius in his mind. Going to the hotel, a winter blizzard shutting the hotel down, having the room, and there in the room, Wendy and Danny, waiting for the ax to fall. It was perfect and he knew any real *Shining* fan would want no less than the full experience — ax and all.

The icing on the cake was locating a vintage typewriter just like Jack used in the movie, then printing a large stack of paper, each filled with the sentence, *"All work and no play makes Jack a dull boy."* He grew more excited with each new idea, and all of them would be the ultimate visit to a nightmare from the mind of Stephen King and the rather perverse take on the story by Stanley Kubrick.

Sitting in his living room made to look like the Gold Ballroom from the movie, he accepted that his life had become about recreating the way he felt when first seeing the movie. In high school he had many visits to a therapist to discuss his obsession with the somewhat upsetting nature of the story — and why he related to it. He saw such sessions with therapists much like Jack Torrance at AA meetings getting help that didn't help at all. There was no particular reason he could think of for his love of all things from the book or movie. He thought them exciting, and deep down he knew he was not like Jack Torrance. He was like Danny. First seeing the movie, he knew what it was like to be Danny riding his Big

Wheel down the hallways all alone, isolated from other children. He was an only child and his parents were socially isolated being farmers. His dad was a drunk and none too kind to him or his mother.

The story was a way to feel hope that he could escape with his mom, battle demons, prevail against forces unseen. It was his father who had demons, and the only demon he saw was his dad when drunk. He believed that the story was one shared by millions of people. A visit to the hotel, surviving the night, that would be helpful therapy to all the other little Danny kids in the world.

His first step was obvious. Reserve the room for a night to experience staying there. Next, find a prime location to hire out Wendy and Danny for people who wanted the full *Shining Experience* when staying at the hotel. Finally, finding actors who looked the part who would become the characters each night. It meant moving to Colorado, up to the mountain place called Estes Park.

There was no hotel called the "Overlook." That was someplace out in Idaho or Montana used for the movie. Stephen King stayed at a rather different looking hotel called The Stanley. It was white, very formal, and not isolated with nothing around it. It was a hotel in a busy little mountain town surrounding it not too far from Denver. The hotel had learned that there was no stopping the interest in staying in the same room number as in the book and movie, and they welcomed the pilgrimage of fans with special room packages and even sold souvenirs. There were days when the town was snowed in, but that was not something that could be guaranteed to anyone reserving the room in winter. He thought about talking to "management" at The Stanley regarding setting up a stand or place in the lobby to hire out a Wendy and Danny, but he heard a voice from his bathroom.

"What? Give them a goldmine? Give them the biggest idea ever? Sure you want to do that?"

Getting up off the couch, he went to his bathroom, frightened as the voice sounded real, not just his imagination.

Inspecting the room, no spirits and no visitors, but he felt there had been a presence there. Suddenly standing frozen and in shock, he realized his feet were wet. There were footprints on the floor, made from water. Running out of the bathroom he realized he had taken a shower just a short while earlier, They were his footprints, not a ghostly visitor although that didn't explain the voice. He realized that his idea was stirring up the spirits, and he smiled. That would be great for business.

No Reservations

Driving up the mountain road he was thinking of how long the road really was. It had been ten years since he came up with the idea to create an "All Work and No Play" weekend experience for extreme fans of *The Shining*. Knowing any business idea would take money, his time had been spent working at a local extended stay hotel learning the hospitality business as a desk clerk. Volunteering to work overtime and extra days, he saved all the money he could, and the lonely hours behind the check-in desk gave him time to plan his ultimate *Shining Experience* as he liked to reference it. The road to such a venture was not without its own scares. He faced demons lurking in the guise of lawyers and rights holders. At first he was frightened of them, but soon knew they were just like the ones in the book. Ghouls preying on weak and fragile minds, not determined like him.

Forming a business, he consulted a lawyer who he thought was a regular Floyd, the bartender. Full of sinister meaning and intent. Calm, mannered, but on "management's" side, not his. His first meeting felt like being at the bar in the Gold Room, empty, and the bar was the one lawyers all belonged to. He wasn't falling for it.

"Jimmy, I understand your idea. I've used as much time as possible to review your business plan, but the free visit is only an hour. So, a few things... well... that may keep you from getting yourself into some serious legal trouble."

Looking at the man, he expected him to take out a bottle of bourbon like Floyd would do and offer him a drink to help soothe his nerves. He waited, and the lawyer continued as he nodded, wanting to hear.

"First, I don't see that you have obtained any form of approval from The Stanley Hotel or from Mr. King. Have you attempted either?"

Shaking his head, Jimmy wondered why that mattered, telling him they had nothing to do with his plan.

"That's true in the sense they aren't partners or investors, but they are the ones who own the names and the intellectual property you wish to use. You'll need their permission. It may be possible as your venture is a form of promoting the hotel, the book and the movie. Even with that, they may require a share of any income you generate in exchange for use of their property."

Looking at him with skepticism, Jimmy wanted to hear why he should pay them anything, or even get their permission.

"First, the hotel is a hotel, and yes, they rent out a certain room number and it's a popular destination. I can't be sure at this moment, but they may have an agreement with Mr. King or some business arrangement even though the hotel in the book is called The Overlook, not The Stanley. It's simply a place Mr. King and his wife were staying at when he came up with the idea. Respecting the reputation of The Stanley Hotel, Mr. King used a different name and only later revealed the inspiration. It was never a true event. He didn't use their name like you would want to. So, the first business is to get an agreement with The Stanley Hotel to use their name, images of the property, along with promoting a tourist attraction using their hotel and reputation. That may not be something they want as they seem to be doing well without it."

Looking at Jimmy, the lawyer could see he was getting irritated so figured it best to finish explaining there was more.

"If you do get their cooperation, there is the matter that you will be using well established characters from Mr. King's book, *The Shining*, and from the movie, *The Shining*, and the likeness of the actors in the movie. Those are from copyrighted materials, meaning the characters, the images of them, what they say and do… those are all owned by Mr. King, and I would guess some by his publisher and the movie studio. You need to license the right to use those likenesses, and that may or not be agreed to. If it is, you would most likely have to pay for the right to profit off Mr. King's invention… his characters. Do you understand?"

The bottle of bourbon was being emptied into an imaginary glass in front of Jimmy, and he wasn't about to take a drink. He sat, staring, then asked what else.

"After those two major hurdles, you would have a certain amount of liability. First, hiring actors means they are employed by you, but exposed to workplace risks. Each visitor may be nice, but you must be prepared, legally, to take responsibility if any visitor hurts them or themselves, accidentally or out of fear or panic in some way. Think about it. You have an ax involved, and a child actor. That is complex as there are workplace laws for children regarding hours and time for schooling. All of this would require some expensive insurance to protect everyone involved, including guests. You open yourself up to lawsuits when you have people recreating a violent scene from the book and movie, so I don't think that will be easy to insure. I hate to down your idea, but these are real issues. I've kept it to these matters, and my services, well, they are quite expensive so I would suggest first pursuing the rights to the use of the hotel and the characters. If you obtain those, then I could help with contracts, employment contracts, and any insurance matters to protect you and all involved. At a minimum, I'd need a retainer of $50,000 to take that on."

Wishing the lawyer had an actual bottle of bourbon and a glass, Jimmy thought a stiff drink may help with the news. He had a simple question.

"I know my free consultation time is about up, but I do have one question. Say I find a woman and her kid to go with me to the hotel, for my own weekend stay, for my own dream of playing out the movie scene just for me. Can any of those hotel or book and movie people stop me from doing that, just for myself?"

Leaning back, the lawyer finally smiled, looking sinister doing so.

"No, not at all if you don't do it as a business of some sort, just you as a guest staying the weekend. I would suggest having a simple agreement with such a woman and her child that it's just a vacation, and you aren't hiring them to act a part. If you have friends who could do it, that would be fine. I see you'd want to post it to social media, and people do that when they stay there, so no issue there. If you find such a posting has others wanting to share such a vacation there, and ask you to arrange it, then it's worth approaching the hotel and Mr. King. If it gets to that point, come back to see me. I'll be here and I'll keep my notes. Consider it a trial run. A test. See how you like it."

Leaving the law office, Jimmy was glad he asked the last question as that meant he could at least go there on his own, not promote it, but find some mom and her kid to play it out and video it all. After posting it on social media and fan sites there may be a bunch of people who'd want to do the same thing, and he could "challenge" them to do what he had done and figure out a way to do it without involving the hotel or King or lawyers. He wasn't going to get lost in the maze.

After his free law consultation, he made a reservation for the room, which was easy to do during the less-busy winter months. Then, he found putting a post on TikTok seeking a mother and child to play the roles from the movie for a TikTok challenge got so many responses he had to turn people away. Many of the woman were far too shapely, and it seemed they were selling subscriptions to a fan site where they showed more than needed for the Wendy role. There were some, living nearby, and he found one woman who was a dead ringer for Shelley Duvall and had a son just the right age. She loved the idea of being part of the posting. His idea had generated lots of interest, and he was dead set on showing the world that his idea was a great one that true fans would love.

After the slow drive up the slippery narrow road up to Estes Park, he learned how crazy the weather in the mountains of Colorado was. Starting out in Boulder, there wasn't any snow. An hour later, up the mountain to Estes Park, it was snowing heavily and people were driving slow and with caution. The area was beautiful. He had never driven up to the Rockies and he was amazed at how large the mountain were. He understood how the location influenced the story. He had arranged to meet the TikTok woman and her boy at a Starbucks in the parking lot next to the Safeway right near The Stanley, and he called to say although going slow, he would be there soon. She told him they were there, and be careful, it looked to be quite a storm brewing.

Going over a final rise in the road he could see the lights of Estes Park ahead of him. The snow and lights from businesses and homes looked far different from the sparse mountainside location of the Outlook in the movie. He knew it wouldn't look the same, but it was a letdown as it was so different. State Trooper cars had their lights flashing ahead and he was stopped and told no roads open past Estes Park, so did he have a place to stay for the night? He assured the Trooper he had his reservation and was waved on.

Having taken a long time to arrive due to the snow, lights from businesses and the city were being turned off and the whole place was looking more like a Stephen King story. The snow created a ghostly mist, the lights glowed and glared. The streets were almost empty as many cars were turned back as people didn't have lodgings or were going past the town. As he drove to the Starbucks, there was only one small SUV in the lot, and he was glad to see the place was still open.

Walking in, he saw a tall, thin woman and a child, and he waved at them, calling out, "Wendy?" She smiled and nodded but looked nothing like Wendy. The boy didn't look much like Danny as he had a crew-cut. As he went to the couch and chairs they were sitting in, he said hello, and that he almost didn't recognize them. The woman smiled, pointing to a bag next to her.

"We have our costumes and wigs. Wait to you see me change to Wendy, and my boy will have you believing he is Danny!"

He took their word for it, and she was quite thin and tall, and did look a bit like Shelley Duvall. The boy sat quietly and looked out the window at the snow. He asked her how she wished to get into costume, and she said it was no problem. They would change in the ladies room. She suggested getting a hot double cocoa as they got into character. After a nod, she took the bag and told the boy to go with her.

Getting a large double hot cocoa, he sat, waiting, and grew excited. He had longed for his stay at the famous hotel, in the famous room, and even better he was going to be there with his own Wendy and Danny. His iPhone was ready to capture it all, the room was paid for, and he had cash for his two cohorts.

Watching, waiting for the door to the ladies room to open, he gasped as Wendy and Danny stepped out. She hadn't been kidding. She looked right out of the movie, and the boy had long hair, brown, and a blank stare while pretending to talk to his hand in the shape like Danny made in the movie. He stood up, smiling, and they walked up to him, a bit cautiously.

"How's the writing going, Jack? You've been at it all day. Ready to have some dinner? I found some cans of peaches in the storeroom — the ones you like…"

Impressed at how convincingly the two had gotten into character, he decided to join in.

"I… keep… telling you not to bug me about… my work! Wendy! When are… you… going to… listen?"

She almost cowered from his tone, saying dinner was all ready, and took Danny by the hand. They all walked to the parking lot, but with the cars now covered in snow, the lot not plowed, she started walking towards the hotel, trudging through the deepening snow. He understood it was a short walk and best to not drive until the roads were cleared. He wasn't used to the snow, and it was deep. The lot surrounding The Stanley was almost empty. The hotel glowed from its room lights shining in the falling snow, now quite heavy. He figured it best to get checked in so the room wouldn't be given away as they were past check-in time, and he'd go back for all their luggage after.

Once inside he could feel the eerie nature of an empty hotel in the winter blizzard. Wendy and Danny, as he now thought of them, stood a distance behind him as he went to the front desk to check in. Waiting behind one counter meant for many clerks, there was a lone man, skinny, balding, wearing wire rimmed glasses and a suspect smile. He nodded as Jimmy walked up to the counter, saying he had been waiting for them.

"Welcome, Mr. Torrance. I am so glad you didn't let the snow stop you and your family from your stay. We've been expecting you and have your room ready. Ah, yes, 237. A fine room for such a nice family…"

The following Monday in Denver, Mr. Davis, the lawyer Jimmy had consulted, was on TikTok looking at Jimmy's video post. He had an email from Jimmy saying he was going to livestream his stay and post it as well, so check it out after the weekend. The lawyer clicked on the one post and it showed Jimmy, talking to the camera, saying he, Wendy and Danny had checked in and showed the room number, 237. He pointed the iPhone camera to the room, looking dark and cold, with Wendy and Danny in the room waiting for him, looking nervous. Jimmy turned the camera back to the hallway and the lawyer heard him gasp, then the sound of two young girls, he was sure, saying they had been waiting for him.

colorado dreamin'

It was a short clip and ended there. He decided to wait as Jimmy's video and may have been deemed unsuitable but could be in demand and released later that week, but it never was. He emailed him, and the emails were never answered. He nodded; glad all had turned out well. He called the hotel, and they assured him that his client had never been a guest. A no-show due to the storm. He smiled, nodding once more.

Finally, he told his secretary, a young thin woman who gave him a knowing look, nodding about his not seeing more than a short clip about Jimmy's visit to 237. She said the next client was waiting to meet, and he told her to send him in.

A man with long shorts and a *Shining* tee shirt came in, telling him he had an idea for a business about spending a weekend at the hotel *The Shining* was inspired by and put his backpack and keys on the desk. The keyring had a room 237 key fob on it. Mr. Davis smiled at him, said that was an interesting idea, but there may be certain liabilities… and risks.

The man, not deterred, said that was why he was there.

the calling

true fiction

For some, there is a call. An irrational need to up and move to a new place for a change. Others move to find people more like themselves, have a job offer, or to be closer to family.

This story is about a young woman who moves to Denver, having no clue as to why. After a series of events that would make a wonderful fantasy story, she discovers why she followed the call to move.

"Mom, I know I'll be far away. I know it doesn't make sense… Yes, yes, yes… I know I have a job and a nice apartment. I don't know why… I just, well, want to…"

Angela was looking at the WalMart medium-sized packing boxes on her small kitchen counter ready to be taped shut. Having packed her fragile dishes and glasses with care, they were the last boxes to be packed. Looking at the counter she was counting them as she had calculated how many moving boxes, along with her few furniture items, would fit in the $19.99-a-day small moving truck she had rented.

"No, I don't know anyone there. No, I'm not running off with some guy you don't know about! C'mon, you know I wouldn't do that. Geez, mom. We talked all about this stuff last night. I know you were crying and dad was yelling and all. What? No! Not because I don't want to be near you! Where do you get such ideas? I told you both if it doesn't work out for any reason, I'll move back. Ah, mom. I'm 25 and I've been doing the same things since I was a kid. Same places, same friends, same everything. If I don't do something, I'll be doing all that the rest of my life. I want to try something new and that's really all. See how I do on my own without someone there helping me or telling me what's best to do. No, I know you just want me to be okay, and not telling me what to do…"

Hearing her mother crying was a moment where she was close to saying she'd unpack everything and stay. The thought shot through her and it was not a good feeling. That was living for everyone else, not for herself. That gave her a certainty she hadn't had until being shook by that realization.

"Mom, I know dad doesn't want to talk to me right now, and I want you to tell him I love him and I am sure he'll be proud of me if I do this. Thank him for taking my car to sell, and for calling the Chevy dealer in Denver after I found the one I liked online and getting me a good deal. Yeah, the truck rental place is just a few blocks from the dealer so no problem there. I already talked to the dealer and they said they helped with new movers all the time and will have everything ready. The apartment? Yep, the lady said it was all ready and has the keys waiting for me. Yes, I'll call along the way. It's just a day's ride and no motel or anything. I have to get off now and get to bed as I leave really early. Yes, the bed's in the little truck. I have my sleeping bag laid out and I'm pretty sure I'm all set. Just a few boxes from the kitchen to load now, then a few little things to put in there when I leave. Okay, I'll call you when I'm on my way…"

Knowing moving away was not going to be easy for her parents, they were worried but actually had been helping her, even if begrudgingly. Being in Scotts Bluff, as much as she loved the ranch-land of Nebraska where she lived all her life, aside from county agency and service sector jobs she didn't see much of a future for herself there. She wasn't cut out to be a cattle inspector, government worker or teacher. She had been working at a community college in admissions, a nice place with nice people, but it wasn't a job she wanted to do the rest of her life. Her coworkers had been there a long time and planned to stay until they retired. Every turn was a dead end. The closest big city was Denver, and being less than a one-day ride from her family, easy to visit for holidays and for them to visit her. It wasn't like moving to New York or Los Angeles. It was close, but a big city. It was full of promise in her mind. She didn't have a job lined up, and that was a concern as she'd be living on savings for a while. The online job listings had companies begging for people to work for them so she felt it best to move there, learn about the city and where a good place to work would be, then take it from there. A bit risky, but she had a confidence things would be okay. She was a hard worker, had good references, personable, and had a degree in business administration which is what most open positions seemed to require.

Waking up the next morning at dawn, her body ached from sleeping on the floor but a hot shower helped. As she was getting dressed the doorbell rang, surprising her. Opening the door, it was her dad standing there with his yard work clothes on.

"Let's get the rest of your stuff in the truck. I'll help you tie it down if it needs it. I brought rope."

Tears ran down her cheeks and she hugged him. Telling him thanks, she saw he was getting misty-eyed as well. Just joyous to see him, she didn't press the sentimental issues and they finished loading the little truck. Closing the driver's side door as she got behind the wheel, he stepped back, smiled, though there was a touch of sadness showing through. He stood in the street waving as she pulled away, The image in the big side view mirror was one she would treasure. It was the faith in her she had prayed for and she was moved he had come to say goodbye.

Reaching the maze of on and off ramps, all under construction, defining the Denver City limits, her Maps app was shouting out commands. Change lanes! Exit ahead! Unused to driving a truck she was holding the steering wheel for dear life. Honking horns at her for driving slow, all manner of cars, pickup trucks, and SUVs passed around her. Knowing she had entered a new world full of people going here and there, she guessed they were probably tired of seeing moving trucks each day bringing new people to the already crowded city.

Having made good time, the car dealer was open until nine. Following the phone commands, she exited and drove to her new apartment. Just as the manager of the complex had promised, waiting was one of the tenants. He was a burly, strong man ready to help her move her things from the truck into the apartment. With his help, in under an hour everything had been moved out of the truck. He helped her assemble her bed frame which was the one thing she'd need right away. Paying him in cash, he assured her he'd be around if she needed more help. Although there were plenty of boxes to unpack, that had to wait. The next step was to pick up her new car and drop off the truck.

Pulling into the truck rental lot, she managed to find the right spot for dropping off a return. Before texting she was there, a man came to read the odometer, check the gas level, then inspected the truck for damage. While he was doing all that, she could see the Chevy dealer a few blocks down Colfax Avenue. She called her salesman saying she was dropping off the truck and would be there soon. He said to stay put, he'd pick her up in her new car. Paying for the truck rental using an app on her phone to sign and pay, she saw a shiny orange Equinox pull into the lot, knowing it was hers.

"Thank you for picking me up. It's so close, I could have walked it."

Nodding, he said it was no problem. With all the paperwork and payments done online he said it would be a good chance to show her how everything worked, make sure she was happy with it, then it was all hers. He added just be sure to drop him off before she headed to the mountains!

Laughing, they both looked past the building at the foothills where the Rockies began.

"Well, having grown up in Nebraska, I'm pretty used to mountains and all as we'd come here for vacations each year. I'm not used to traffic, though."

Dropping him off, she rubbed the leather seats, smelled the new car scent, then wirelessly paired her iPhone with the infotainment system of the car. It was her first night in the big city. Before leaving the car lot she got out, took a picture of the car with the mountains in the background showing a pretty sunset, then texted it to her parents. She said she'd call later after she ate and got back to the apartment.

New car, new apartment, new life. It was exactly what she had wanted and making it all happen was easier than she thought it would be. She recalled being told by the car salesman and the lady who managed her apartment complex they had things worked out for new movers. Picking up what they were saying in a nice way, the message was there were endless people moving there regularly, and it did seem that they knew just how to help a person new to the area. She wondered how many like her stayed, making it their home. Knowing it would be different for each person, such thoughts left her mind as she found a Kings Sooper grocery store, getting a frozen pizza for dinner and a few other food essentials.

The next day she unpacked all the boxes. She was impressed as her apartment was new, though expensive. After long calls to family and friends she found herself sitting on her bed looking online at job listings, then at assorted things to do around the Denver area. Finding many outdoor adventure articles, she only bookmarked them. She hadn't moved only to do the endless activities featured in the "What to do in Denver" articles. Any such activity was for the future with new friends. Searching for ways to meet people when new in town, she wasn't interested in the night life though there was plenty of it. Again, better to go to such places with good friends, not as a single young woman alone.

That's when she heard a "call" from out of nowhere. It told her to type "writer meetings" into the search bar. One of her dreams was to complete a book she started when in high school. She hadn't know any other people interested in writing books and she hoped she could meet some writers in her new city life.

Hitting the Enter button, up came a listing that was the next "call" to her. Listed was a group for new writers. It was free and nearby. Looking it over, it wasn't a dating site. It was part of a large meeting site where people with similar interests could find each other and meet at a coffee shop or library to share their hobbies or interests. It seemed perfect. Eyes opening wide, there was a meeting the next morning, Sunday, at a coffee shop with eight people attending. Reading each of their brief bios, looking at their pictures, most were working on their first book. It was exactly why she moved to a larger city. She wanted to meet people like herself, interested in things she was interested in too.

Signing up, she hit the RSVP button, and with that she was part of the *Rocky Writers Group*. Her picture and bio were up for others to see, and she took a screenshot of the group hoping to remember the names against the faces. Opening Word on her laptop, she pulled up her book file and began reading it. Worrying that it may be a bit silly as it was begun when in high school, she spent the rest of the night reading it — something she hadn't done for months. Unsure of her writing skills, she hadn't shown it to anyone, afraid they'd put it down or dismiss her effort. Finishing what she had written so far, she smiled. It was a good story. It needed some editing, but she had a sense the other writers would understand. Writers start somewhere, and at different times in their lives.

The group had members close to her age, some older, some younger. It would be interesting. Finally, people she could talk to about something she loved doing but didn't think anyone else would understand.

Walking into the coffee shop the next morning with her laptop in hand, she saw a woman who looked to be about 30 sitting at a table typing away on a large laptop. She recognized her as the group organizer, and went over to ask if the table was for the writing group.

"Yes, it is. Oh, you just signed up last night. Great! I'm so happy you did. Hey, get some coffee or something. Food here is great. It's early so we can talk a bit and get to know each other."

Feeling instantly welcome, she was elated. Going up to get a cup of chai tea, she was back at the table and chatting away with the woman.

"Well, I'm Rocky, and I started this group. All good people, and I keep hoping for more to join. It'll be where we'll all introduce ourselves as you are new, and you to tell us about yourself. So, is this your first writers' group?"

Smiling, nodding, sipping tea, she was joyous to be asked if she was a part of a "writers" group.

"Oh, more than that. This is my first week in Denver, and yes, my first ever meeting with other writers."

Clearly happy to hear all of that, Rocky smiled, saying she had only lived in the Denver area for a year so knew how it was. Adding many of the writers were also new to Denver, she'd have a lot in common with them.

"So, Angela, here for work?"

"No. Just decided one day I wanted to move and be on my own. Be in a new place. Maybe meet writers, find a good job. So, big risk, I know. That's what my parents keep going on about."

Looking at her with admiration, Rocky said that was wonderful and she'd be there to turn to if she needed any help. As she was saying that, two writers walked up, put coffee cups down and joined them. Soon, the table was full, all there saying hi to each other, then introducing themselves to her. Looking at her phone, Rocky called everyone to attention, saying time to start, and go around and do short introductions and talk about their writing projects. Amazed at how respectful each one there was, they each said who they were, what they did for a living, what genre they were writing in, and the status of their works in progress.

Listening intently, she learned people there had things in common. Six of them belonged to another meeting group for gamers. That tied in with their writing genre being fantasy stories which was part of their love of gaming. Half the gamers were women, which surprised her as she had never played Xbox or done any gaming. It interested her as they sounded passionate about the stories they were writing. The gamers were all under 30 and had grown up playing video and board games.

The next person had just started writing. He was drafting an outline of a dark urban fantasy. He was in his late 30s, saying he loved reading such books and longed to write one of his own, was happy to have started, and the group was wonderfully supportive.

Rocky was next, saying she had completed one book, working on her second, and that she hadn't found a publisher but wasn't going to get discouraged as finding an audience was the hard part. All nodded in agreement.

The last one to introduce himself was sitting next to her. He was older than the others there. Rocky looked at him, putting two fingers to her eyes in a "V" shape, then pointing them to him in a mock warning to behave and she was keeping her eyes on him. He smiled at her, shrugging, then looking at Angela.

"I've been commanded to reel myself in during introductions. Rocky is reminding me. I'm not working on my first book, don't play games, so a bit different from the others, I guess."

Rocky made the fingers from her eyes to his tease again.

Looking at the interchange, Angela looked at him, asking if he wanted to be a writer and was that why he joined the group. He looked into her eyes and he was not like anyone she had met before. He was completely sincere, gentle yet strong in his manner. He kept his eyes to hers as he answered.

"Yes, I want to be a writer, but no, not working on my first book. I'm on number 57."

Giving him a stern look, Rocky sighed, but he ignored the taunt. He calmly waited and watched Angela's expression.

"57 books! Are any of them published?"

Without changing expression, gentle and sincere in his gaze as he answered, she felt that feeling of being in a different place, of being "called" there for a reason.

"Yes. All of them. The first 45 by the big publishing houses. Now by a publishing company I've owned all my life. Not exactly self-published, but as I own the company, I do say I'm self-published now."

Cutting in, Rocky said yes, he's written lots of books and it would take all day to list them, so maybe best to look them all up on Amazon, but now it was time for her to introduce herself.

It was hard for her to stop looking at the man who was still kindly looking into her eyes. She felt as if he was learning all about her, or already knew more about her than anyone else ever would. It was a comforting feeling, one of complete acceptance.

Pulling her eyes away, she looked round the table and took a deep breath.

"I'm Angela, and wow, what a nice group to be a part of. I don't have my first book published yet, by anyone, including me! I just moved here from Scotts Bluff, in Nebraska. You know, where all the cattle are. I used to work for a community college doing admissions, and one day felt it was time to move someplace where I could meet writers, maybe get a job doing that too. It's a big change for me. I've been working on my first book a long time. With family and work and all that, it's hard to write too. I'm almost finished, so really excited about that, and why I joined this group. I hope to learn how others work all day and write too. Oh, and to make writer friends."

Meeting with nods and comments that many would be happy to read what she's done or be a reviewer, she told everyone she'd be happy to do the same for them. Feeling welcome, no longer alone, she smiled and knew she had moved for that very reason. To be with others like her.

Rocky tapped the table, telling everyone social time was up, no more chatting until after the writing session, one hour, then lunch for those who could make it. Then they could talk about anything they wanted. Suddenly keys were clicking and the group was focused on writing and respecting that others needed quiet to do the same. Opening her laptop, she leaned over and asked the man with all the published books what his full name was. He whispered in her ear as not to not disturb others, saying his name was Lee Michael. Nodding at him, she watched as he casually typed away, never looking at the keys, eyes closed as he typed.

Opening Wikipedia, she typed in his name and found him listed. His picture was on a long page of information detailing his books and other well-known works including photography and film making. He was famous but had dropped from public view about fifteen years back. His history read like a work of fiction. He had a long string of best sellers, taught PhD writing and language, photographed famous magazine covers, and produced movies she had seen. There he was, next to her, listening to her with interest, with a group of people just starting out or who hadn't written much yet. Wondering what happened and why was he there like a first time writer, she had the feeling of being called. That she had moved, the move not making any sense, only to meet him. She stopped. Stunned. She realized that was what all her changes had been about. To take her to the coffee shop, sit with a group of first time writers, and to meet him.

As she thought that, he opened his eyes and looked into hers. She had been looking over at him so they had eye contact. He nodded ever so slightly and she realized he knew exactly what she was thinking. He leaned over and whispered in her ear again.

"It's the same for me."

It was overwhelming and real. She looked up each of his books. He had books that had sold millions of copies. Novels, self-help, how-to books, all top sellers for years and years. His more recent books weren't best sellers and didn't even have book reviews. After looking at them, she looked over at him. He titled his head, shrugged his shoulders, and smiled. He was saying, without words, he could care less.

The writing hour went by fast. Rocky said thanks to everyone, then asking if they'd care to join her down the block for lunch. Half had to do other things, but Lee Michael said he'd like to, and Angela, in a daze trying to absorb the last hour, nodded yes, she wanted to go too.

Sitting in a large booth for six, the lunch was friendly, fun and casual. Rocky complemented Lee for not taking up all their time talking about his past. He said he didn't wish to be punched or kicked out of the group. Rocky turned to Angela, saying she didn't believe a word of his wild stories, but he was a very good at critiques, so she let him stay part of the group. Having just read all about him online and that all his books were on Amazon, she thought to ask about why she teased him, but sensed it was a running joke and perhaps Rocky hadn't looked up his listings. It was all part of the mystery that day, of that meeting.

She was sitting next to Lee. He was interacting with the others in a casual way, giving her looks and soft smiles during the meal and conversations. He asked the ones there about their cars or apartments, or if they saw a movie or read some book. Thinking to herself about the interactions she was in a state of wonder. How could all the aspiring writers there not be asking questions of a man who had done everything they dreamed of doing, and more. He probably could guide them to success, or introduce them to publishers or agents, yet not one person at the meeting or the lunch asked him anything about writing or publishing.

At first wondering if he had been asked such things before and not been interested in sharing, she didn't pick that up. Rocky's eye taunt seemed to be a message of don't lecture about how to do things. She suddenly knew that was what her message was: Don't share his knowledge or success. She thought that strange, wondering why not??

She started thinking of being on social media when she was longing to learn about book writing prior to moving to Denver. There were accomplished writers who had few followers, no comments or questions and not one of them were influencers. There were all kinds of young writers, still on their first sentence, posting about how they had to go get coffee before they could write a single word, many asking for help, saying each day they were stuck, or how could they possibly get their book done when they had to strip naked to make a selfie to post. It hit her that those were the ones with huge numbers of followers, comments and likes. Not because they wrote anything or were actual writers, but because they were good at social media. She had wasted so much time reading nonsense about how hard it was to write, but had never read the ones from authors who actually had written and were happy to share their knowledge.

People in the writer's group were actually working on books, so not like social media, but they had a person who could at least be an inspiration and they hardly paid attention to him. It started making sense. Just like she had moved, making her own way, they were on their journey, and they had to do it on their own. It wasn't how she would be. She felt a connection with Lee. It was destined that they meet. That's what she felt, and he had whispered he felt the same calling

As lunch ended, she whispered to him, asking if he wanted to have some ice cream or dessert. He smiled, and nodded. The others left, and she walked down the street with him and they found an ice cream parlor where they talked for three hours.

"Lee, I kept wondering why someone who has done so much was in a group of people who don't even want to talk about things you've done. I felt bad for you, Rocky pointing at you like that to tell you to keep from sharing things..."

Laughing, he nodded, saying it was interesting, but for a reason.

Angela just stared at him, wanting to know the reason. He knew what her stare was about.

"Yeah... I usually write a book in a week, sometimes longer if I'm flying all over. That can be intimidating, and I know that. I have time to write as I'm a full-time author. Mostly I like to do things that help people. That called me away and I stopped writing for about 15 years. I had a mission, far away, very spiritual. That was more important than books at the time. But, now I'm back and I've started writing again. I realized I would meet someone special. A kindred spirit. Writes to say something, not only to make money or post online about it and all that. I had a knowing, as I call those things, that if I joined this group I'd meet the person who would change my life, and I would change theirs. I don't think it's good to hold back things that need to be said, or anything important. I looked at you today, and I knew you were why I joined. To meet you."

Trying hard not to let her mouth hang open in wonder, she stared at him, realizing she had never met anyone so aware, so able to understand her. To say what anyone else would be afraid to say. The truth. He was not like anyone she had ever met. He said all the things she was thinking inside of herself.

"Lee. Wow. Everything you just said is completely true. It's why I moved here. To meet you, just like you said about me. I mean, like, can this be real? I mean, how can this be?"

Looking at her, he had a look of comfort that made her feel safe and wonderful. He shrugged, then leaned over to answer her.

"Does it matter? Does that need an answer? I'm sitting here, thinking okay, it was meant to be. Accept it. I have no questions. I have you, here, talking to me, looking at me. I don't see anyone else here from the group, never have. All I have is an answer. You are why I joined the group and showed up each week. And why you found this group and showed up. I know that's the answer. It's because it is. It's why we are sitting here right now. Does that help a bit?"

Leaning forward, her eyes to his, she nodded. They stared at each other. She agreed completely.

"It answers questions I've had all my life, actually. Those have all been answered. I'm not sure what finding each other means right now. I know it's more than books and things. I feel important. I feel understood. I feel good for the first time in my life about who and what I am. I have a question. What are you writing about? I mean, well, right now."

"About a girl who has questions that have no answers. She doesn't know why, but an answer appears from out of nowhere."

As amazing as it sounded, as improbable as it would be to anyone else, it made perfect sense to her.

He asked her about the book she had been writing for so long. Unlike all the times she had been cautious or embarrassed to describe it, all that vanished and she told him.

"Well, it's a fairy tale, really. The style is, at least. It's about a little girl who lived in a strange land, in a tower with a moat around it. There was nothing pretty past the moat and the tower. Only fields and farms, far as she could see. So, with nothing to visit, nothing to see, she stayed in her tower room. When young she was content looking out the window of her room. It was nice because she was a princess as girls are always princesses in fairy tales. It's a rule! She began wondering if it was just endless fields forever and ever. Her life was looking out that window, always looking, never seeing anything. As she grew older, she became sad knowing her whole life would be nothing, like the emptiness all around the tower…"

Pausing, she saw Lee was deeply immersed in her story, often closing his eyes to visualize it, she was sure. He looked at her as she paused.

"And you wrote that in your late teens? That is perfect. How long does that go on in the story?"

Closing her eyes to think, she opened them, saying at least a hundred pages. He asked why so long to describe one thing.

"Whoa. Bam! You know your stuff. I read you were a professor and taught grad writing classes. Excellent question. I remember thinking about that. I kept writing all about the tower, the grain flowing with the wind, the empty roads, how nobody visited, how she had no one to talk to. I thought about how is someone going to understand how isolated, lonely and alone she was if I didn't explain the endless monotony… the feeling of each day being so empty. So, I tried to make the reader feel like the princess, getting more and more upset about how terrible being isolated was. I didn't think much more than that. I only knew I wanted to explain how it felt, and make the reader feel that."

His head nodding gently, he said he that was the best way to do it. That's exactly the way to explain what happens next, then asked what does happen next. Her eyes lit up, and her face grew excited.

"Like I said, a fairy tale. Pure fantasy thing, really, so I could have amazing things happen. One day she's staring out the window like she always had, and floating in the air in front of her was an Angel."

Waiting for a reaction, Lee nodded, fully understanding the story. She smiled, letting him know she appreciated his understanding.

"Of course the girl prayed at the tower chapel each morning and there were ornate paintings of Angels there, but the Angel wasn't anything like Angels in those paintings. The Angel was so different. Beautiful beyond what could be possible, but not just in looks. The Angel was beauty, I mean. Not just beautiful. Beauty. What beauty is. What was more amazing was when looking at the Angel she couldn't see the empty horizon or fields. The Angel had wings so large they filled the whole sky, blocking out everything making her feel trapped. I wrote a whole chapter about how big the wings were, and how wonderful it was to look out a window and see beauty. Endless, perfect beauty. For the first time, ever. The Angel gave her hope. Showing her things she kept looking out the tower window for, but never saw.

Lee looked at her. He just stared. Again, he told her that was perfect. It was perfect as it was true. He said to continue, he was in awe. She didn't pause, even with such praise. She had waited for this day so long.

"That's when I took a long break from writing. I had graduated from school, got my job and felt trapped and hopeless, like in the story. Then, one day, and I can't recall any reason why, I started writing again. So, the princess, she realizes that hey, it's an Angel, and an Angel can help her. So, she calls out, asking to see more things past the fields all around the tower. Other places that are different. The Angel still hadn't said anything, but the wings were much more than feathers. They're like a movie screen. The wings started showing happy people walking in forests, fishing in rivers, dancing, families eating dinner, riding horses, and all kinds of places. Hills and valleys. Little farms with animals, oceans, mountains. All things she couldn't even imagine. She's crying the whole time, all the visions so wonderful, all things she would never see in the tower. She falls to her knees, crying, sobbing from it all. The Angel there, only floating outside the window."

Lee was excited, his expression showing it. He said that was wonderful and asked her to tell the rest.

"Lee, just a bit more as that brings me to now and wanting to finish the book. I left it where she finally stands up, wipes her tears, begging the Angel to take her away to all those places, To save her. I left it where the Angel lifts its giant wings straight up, allowing her to see the endless fields again, which makes her sick, and she's heaving and vomiting. She keeps crying out, wanting the Angel to take her away, over and over. Again, the

Angel says nothing but looks to the road instead. The long endless road in front of the tower. Not saying a thing, she realizes the Angel is saying that all those things are out there, down the road. But she won't be carried or helped, she has to go down the road on her own. But, still not sure, she asks if that's what the Angel meant. The Angel begins gently flapping the wings, the fields are rippling from the wings creating a gust, and without a word the Angel rises up into the sky. She's in the tower, watching the Angel, and her hopes… well, fly away."

Sitting there, looking at Lee, she had a surprised expression. She felt the same way as when she wrote that part. It was the first time she understood the story she had written. It was a shock. Just telling it to someone finally helped her understand what her story was really about. She looked up at him.

"Well, no need to say it. I've always read first novels are autobiographical. I didn't agree. I just didn't know it was about me. Well, until now."

He sat looking at her. It was a look of knowing, of understanding. It was what she had longed for. She smiled at him, telling him just telling her story to him made her understand it. She thanked him for hearing a young girl's fantasy. He shook his head, his eyes kinder still.

"Well… I did hear a story… but not a fairy tale or fantasy. I heard what you endured, how you felt, what life was like for you. I heard you tell how one day an answer appeared, and the path was clear. So, are you still in the place you were enduring all your life? Did you stay in the tower? Where are you? Right now? Today?"

Angela started to cry, gently as she was in public. Taking the napkin her spoon was on, she wiped at her tears, then she was able to talk.

"No. Not anymore. I left my world… my parents… friends, people at work. They all said it was stupid to move to Denver. What was in Denver for me? Then, and I don't know what did it, I knew there was a road out, and I left. And now, I'm here, I'm being treated like the writer I am… No, way more than that. The person I am. And, I'm sitting here with you. That's the part I'm crying about…"

His hands were on the table, folded. It was a small ice cream parlor table, and they were close to each other to not talk too loud about such things in public. Angela put her hands over his, feeling a wave of elation ripple through her at the touch. She looked at his hands, then finally looked up into his eyes.

"So, are you the Angel?"

A year later Angela opened an email from her book agent having a jpeg of the *New York Times* Best Seller list attached. On top, in the number one spot, was her first novel. It had been the number one seller for two months. The agent had included a link to videos of interviews with her on several network morning shows where she was asked, over and over, if she thought having a non-fiction novel about an encounter with a divine entity at the top of the bestselling fiction list was divisive, only to sell books, unfair to people who didn't share her faith? Was she deceiving people, writing fiction but actually preaching?

She could only feel sorry for them and see their need to doubt her.

In every interview, in print, online and on broadcasts, she was asked that same question over and over. Her answer was always the same.

colorado dreamin'

"Angels in Denver isn't faith-based, it's inspirational. Yes, I wrote it as a story, but it's not fiction. I'm deeply saddened how media — the press — dismisses faith and Angels by saying it's fictional and not based on what I know to be true. Again, my book is my story, not some fantasy. I never said it's fiction. My publisher never said that. The book jacket doesn't say that. Media is saying that. They can't stand people who have a dream, or hope, or have faith. Do your job and speak true. Since you won't say it, I will. I want everyone to know this. I was called to Denver, but it could be anyplace people find their life, not only Denver. So, for anyone who opens their heart, one day an Angel will show up when you're ready, and you know what? You'll go wherever your faith in yourself may be. That can be right where you are, or someplace else where you belong. You'll see there's an endless stream of people going with you. It's not a "fantasy" like media wants to label it. Want to know what it is? Quote me on this."

"It's a calling."

there are some stories best told using pictures

take a look at colorado through a different lens

the fantasy
and reality
of colorado

a photo story
by mick bland

blucifer
welcomes you

the strangeness can be fun

Flying to Denver for a first visit to Colorado is filled with excitement. Arriving at Denver International Airport provides a different look at the Old West. Long a topic of conspiracy theorists, DIA has some truly unusual things to see. From symbology carved into walls, strange sculptures, UFO images hidden in places, to stories of a world of mystery underneath the airport. It's all probably only a play on myths… or is it? Could it be they are trying to tell us all something? What is a gargoyle sitting in a suitcase doing in an airport? And there's Blucifer watching everyone come or go from the one road in or out of DIA. A blue, vein-popping fully exposed stallion with glowing red eyes. Well, I'm sure it's all in fun. Maybe!

colorado dreamin'

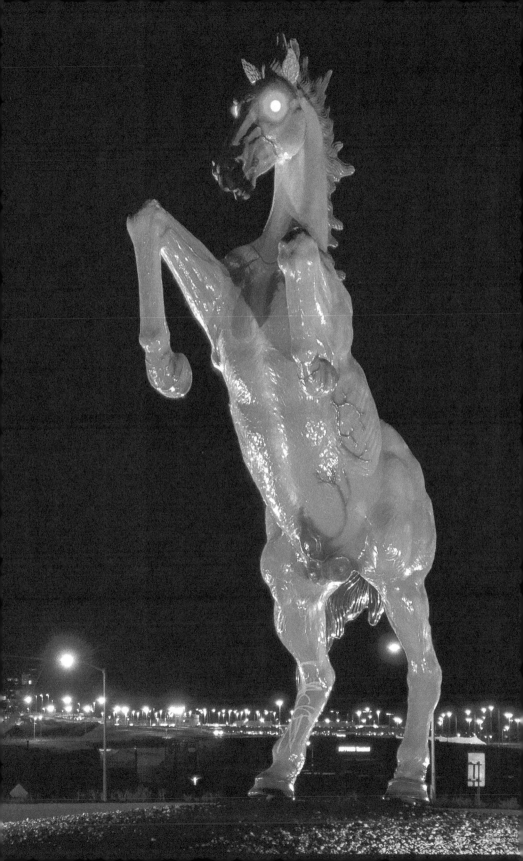

mountains all around us
denver you astound us

denver is in the plains

While it is true Denver is in Colorado, and it is always pictured in tourism pictures showing the glorious Rockies as part of the Denver skyline, well… Denver is actually in the Great Plains and hardly has a hill or even an impressive city skyline. True, it's a short ride to the "foothills," then a short ride to some real mountains, but Denver is located just East of the Rockies; not in them. If you stand a certain way, look between big box stores and it's not a smog alert warning day, then, yes! You can see some Rockies in the distance! Or, like in the pictures here, maybe not. The good news is Denver offers the best of both worlds. Live in a city with all the stuff cities have (traffic, pollution, expensive housing) and be under an hour away from majestic mountains. Well, that's if traffic isn't at a standstill headed out of Denver to the ski resorts full of Wranglers or Suburbans rented from the UFO visitors from other worlds at Denver International Airport.

colorado dreamin'

from forests to mountains colorado is truly beautiful

the john denver songs are right

Once you pass the tourist traps and the ski resorts, there are places where you can see nature the way it has been since long before humans arrived. If you get off the Interstate, find a lonesome trail and have your backpack not too heavy, you can be one with nature and wildlife. The Rocky Mountains offer a diverse landscape, and the beauty is that it's not anything like most people expect. More than snow-capped peaks, the mountains can be bare rocks or almost black covered with endless pine trees. Lakes with great fishing are over two miles above sea-level, and they are pristine and reflect the landscape and the open sky. Above you, hawks soar, birds sing. Ahead may be elk grazing on grasses while chipmunks taunt them with their might. The air is thin, and at night you are welcomed by a sky far from city lights showing you stars and galaxies, all smiling and singing a song found only where few go, but all dream of. This is why Colorado has a mountain range on its license plates. It's beautiful.

wildlife
that's what animals call us

they aren't the ones out of control

Long before people arrived, Colorado belonged to animals large and small. Elk, deer, bear, cat, moose, bison, squirrel, snake, birds of prey, birds preyed upon, fox, and long ago, dinosaurs. When you live in the Rockies far from urban areas, those amazing animals still roam. They are so different from us. They hunt for food, they have fights. The doe deer have fawns, bears roam with their cubs, the owls feast on little creatures in the night. They don't take more than they need, and they live without fast food chains or highways. They don't tear down trees to build housing or big box stores. Watching bulldozers clear land for a strip mall, you'll see rabbits and chipmunks running as their homes are being destroyed with nowhere to run to. We live on their land. We are still an imperialist army taking all ahead of us and killing for sport, not food. Colorado has many survivors of the invasion of mankind. What *we* call wild animals.

colorado dreamin'

trout fishing in colorado
a throwback experience

sport and dinner

Fishing is one of the expectations of Colorado. Streams and lakes fed from snow melting off mountain peaks filled with freshwater fish are part of being one with nature and doing what animals and humans both do. Fish. Hiking, setting up camp… those are magic moments when it's just you, your flyrod, and mountains and sky surrounding you as you find dinner in the waters so blue. Most who fish understand to keep what they catch to eat, then throw back the ones who won't be eaten. It's you and the water. You and the fish. It's more than sport, it's art. The dream of Colorado is beautiful day, a gentle breeze, a calm creek, river or mountain lake with no boats roaring past as the fish take the lure, bite, and you reel in a meal. Animals hunt and fish, and we do too. Now, we hunt with DSLRs and our trophies are stunning pictures hung with pride at office or home, or one or two fish cooking on an open fire.

hiking and camping
where no human has gone before

if you can hike a bit camping is wonderful

You can live the fantasy of camping in nature under the stars, far from others, eating your fresh catch cooked on a fire. The reality is that you may not be able to start a fire as much of the state has a fire ban most times. The forested areas are not what people expect. No paved campsites, no septic or electric hookups, not really for weekends with the camper, Weber kettle grill and DirecTV hooked up. There are tourist campsites if you need any of those, but you'll be a few feet from dozens of other campers and noise. If you are physically fit, you can hike far into a national or state park where camping is permitted, and find a place quiet and isolated to have the fantasy camping experience. A simple tent you carried on your back, sleeping bag, a few utensils… prepare dinner and you're all set. The forest around you has new, old, and dead trees. The forest had fires before we got here. It just seems to burn down more with us around.

local attractions
fantasy most real

the hotdog stand and more

Once you live in Colorado, most likely you'll be in Denver. If you don't want to go hiking, biking, camping, skiing or climbing you can hang at places the locals hope will be kept secret for locals only. That may be a bit tricky for places like Bailey or Pine a bit South and West of Denver. There's a hotdog stand shaped like a hotdog that locals cherish and a hidden treasure. But… next to those towns is Conifer where the creators of *South Park* are from. They included the hotdog stand in *South Park* and now it's famous all over the world. Colorado is full of such tourist havens, and it's fun to visit them for a selfie or two. Once living here there are less touted favorites like old movie houses and wildly fun eateries like Casa Bonita where you eat burritos and watch cliff diving inside a few feet from your table. Well… Gosh. That place was bought and is being renovated by the guys who created *South Park*. Well, they are two locals who know what people want to see: Dogs and dives.

MAYAN
THE WHALE
BABY RUBY
AFTERSUN
ANT-MAN AND THE WASP
QUANTUMANIA
2/17
EVERYTHING EVERYWHERE
OF SADNESS

urban fantasy
emissions and empty trains

denver and the no carbon footprint crusade

The fantasy of living in Denver is different than the reality regarding clean air and public transportation. The pictures here show empty electric trains in rush hour. Built to help reduce pollution and make Denver an environmentally conscious showplace after tearing down housing, spending a fortune, promoting riding a train rather than driving pickups, Wranglers or Outbacks, the trains are most often empty and the roads are full of traffic standing still, polluting the air and wasting energy. The highways to ski resorts are jammed in the winter, and the train from the airport to downtown Denver takes backseat to ride services or rental cars. It may have been better to build electric trains to the ski resorts and the hotdog stand, but nobody will ever admit the trains are not used or reducing the pollution hanging over the city of mile-high SUVs and pickups.

colorado dreamin'

the fantasy
the reality

sometimes a picture says it all

little big one

There is a peculiar phenomenon regarding people new to living in Colorado.

A small green and white sticker looking just like the famous mountain landscape license plate Colorado has used since before there were even cars! The sticker doesn't have letters and numbers. It says, "NATIVE."

Going into a gas station store where they are often sold, I saw a person ahead of me buying one. Walking up to the counter, the clerk looked at the person walking out to their car and said, "Probably just moved here." People think living in Colorado is special, and it is. That moment started me wondering about who lived here first.

As one roams the forests of Colorado you are never alone.

Long before foolish big ones came with their wagons and wicked ways; long before big ones who had been there before the ones with wagons and wicked ways who lived in caves and walked hunched over, few had respect for the forest and woodland creatures; long before any who thought they were big and we were small, know we were here, and still are.

Wondrous we be, but sadly we no longer let our wonder be seen or known. Big ones, oh, they be wicked in their ways and no live like we faeries live. It be our nature to think kind of all beings having life. Even the eagle and the owl, the fox, and also cats who prey on wee animals most new. All give us kind words and know we were most special. The forest is a place of many wonders and has life of its own, as do wee faeries and woodland creatures.

It be true that inside any creature there is hunger to live, and large creatures eat the small, small eat the smaller. All accept what large beasts do because it be their nature. Know none eat more than needed, and none eat only for pleasure.

But know that none, not the hawk, the wolf, or any in this special place eat faeries, and we no eat them. We eat honey made by sweet bees, bark falling from trees, berries fallen to ground round us, but nothing that moves on its own or grows to the sky. There be no need for we have all that does not move on its own, and we give thanks to any food we gather, and those who gave such gifts.

Ah, but know big ones no be like woodland creatures, trees, plants, tiny bugs or things that crawl at night. Big ones, oh, they take any they wish to eat and take more than they need. They no give thanks, and I be hiding in bush many times watching, and some big ones smile as they take life. I hear them boast they be mighty and strong, and all things they take be weak, having no feelings or mind. Big ones take, no give, and they are to be wary of, which we are.

Hawthorne, me sweet true love, called out to me long ago when she saw first big ones coming to mountain where we have lived since all began.

"Birch, come! It be things most strange. I must be dreaming for this no can be!"

Crouching under bush, a dense one, there be Hawthorne looking to a clearing at a sweet fawn we had met but only a moon before that day.

Tinder be her name, and she be golden brown with white spots, gentle and kind. I crouched next to Hawthorne, moving a leaf to see what she saw and feared, shaking so. There be Tinder, laying on her side, a branch from a tree stuck into her slender neck, red stuff, life, inside flowing out neck, pouring her life away. At the end of the stick there be feathers, but we had never seen a bird that looked like that branch, so straight, in the neck of a young friend.

I knew such sight was like none faeries had ever seen and why Hawthorne hid in bush. Glad I was to be with her in bush knowing what she saw. I too saw the reason Tinder be laid low. There be thing most strange at edge of clearing. A thing we could only call big one. A creature we then hoped never to come our way. It walked upright on hind legs like faeries, but it be no faerie. It be huge, had no twinkle in its eyes, no love for sweet fawn Tinder in its heart. We saw true it had bad intent glowing from within.

The big one wore a vine tangled with feathers round its neck and wore the flesh of elk to cover its body. Hawthorne looked at me, showing her worry and fear of the thing. I held finger up to me mouth meaning to no make a sound, and we watched. The big one went to Tinder, then with strange carved rock began taking her apart after hanging her with vines on a tree branch high above its head. First taken was Tinder's fine skin, then red parts under. It was too much for us to watch. Hawthorne was crying, and so was I. The big one smiled as it took the sweet thing apart and we knew it enjoyed owning the life of Tinder.

That was a new day. The day of big ones. Since, they have never stopped coming, no, and never stopped their need to take life. Creatures, trees, plants — all that could no do same harm to them. Know they only be big, but no bold like Hawthorne or me, and they fear bears, cats, or any mighty woodland creature. They take only the weak, never the strong.

Trees be next. Trees be giants, true, but are kind, having no way to stop big ones. Soon, trees fell, burned to cook things that once lived, many torn apart. With branches, leaves, the wee ones living in them all taken away, all that be left of trees be sticks to make strange dwellings, all square, with fires in them burning things once living. More and more trees fell to make more and more strange places where big ones lived. More trees, never stopping, all for boxes to put more big ones in them.

Since that first day, they have never stopped coming. Hawthorne and I hide in bush, hear big ones brag forest, and all in it, were made by giant big one in sky, just for them. They said loud our place is theirs. They take all they want, never giving anything but death to the gentle ones here since time began.

Soon after making their boxes, they took small trees and made cages to keep birds and cows from roaming, using their eggs and milk, then tearing them apart, putting them on their fires to eat them.

All in forests in all places learned a new thing. Fear. All any creature in forest could do is hide if there was place such to find in time. There was no stopping big ones from finding all gentle creatures. They took wolves, no longer wolves, using them to sniff out creatures that hid, and the wolves, not wolves, would bite a fox or small creature downed by pointed sticks or clubs, carry the poor thing to big ones and drop them at their feet.

So it began, was, and has never stopped. The forest, once home to all manner of life, is now home to big ones. There are many more born or coming from afar each moon, hunting woodland creatures, killing and eating them. Much of the forest, once home of elder trees, changed to nothing but grasses, all trees taken down, used to make flames or boxes. It makes sense none to us faeries, and it be no place for us. Big ones now be in all places we know, and we know not where to find new homes for our friends.

Hawthorne and I have lived since all things started but know we can end like poor Tinder if found by the stick of big ones. One poke, one swing of mighty club, we stop being what we are. Alive. Big ones will never understand the wonder we be. We too learned to hide, looking for places to live where no big ones can go. We learned there be few places big ones will not go, and they take all places they see. We learned the strange tongue they speak long ago, and we hear their plans. Some of them have seen faeries in other lands. They know of us, wishing to capture us.

That must never be.

We are not ones to own, put in cages, or display as prize. We are no to be harmed, for that be bad for any who harm us. Any harming faerie will soon wither and fade from life, the price they would pay taking ours. When we hide, we do more than protect ourselves, we protect big ones as well from such fate. We no be like them, and wish no harm to any living thing, even them. It is our way.

For time long, Hawthorne and I lived in hollow of mighty tree on mountain so high air be too thin for big chests. We knew such climb be hard one for big ones. There be little dark soil to plant seeds in. It be good place for us as high place, air thin, soil none, is no harm for us.

One day, not long ago, we heard voices and strange sounds. Hawthorne and I went to find what made such noise, and we both gasped, again, like the first time we saw big ones. Using things no like their wagons and carts, the new things were not natural. We heard them be called earth movers by big ones riding them. With effort none, the earth movers pulled down trees, dug out mountain rocks, made dwellings large and mighty, and paths, black and hard, so their earth movers would no sink into ground. After dwellings be made, we saw new terror. Big ones came out of boxes carrying thunderous fire sticks we had never known before, and downed all creatures from afar, taking heads to hang inside the boxes. We could see into boxes through holes they loved to stand by, looking for us faeries, we be sure. We feared their thunder sticks.

More than any other worry, we feared the truth there be ones who could do any such sadness to the land, trees, woodland creatures, fish, birds above, and even to each other — and would never learn no such harm need be done.

The forest was no longer true. It became sad place filled with big ones who knew not how life was precious, how little they knew, and how much they could no see. They were blind, not blind. They could see helpless creature and take its life, but could no see life inside they took.

The days of faeries was no more. Hawthorne and I knew only faeries could stop them. It is known by all but big ones that faeries have small forms, big hearts, love for those who are good, and wish only to be most wondrous and lovely to behold by any ones true of heart. It be true all in forest left faeries alone, never thinking us food even though a wee squirrel could feast on us for we be so small. We have a way, with a power in our will, that can do things none other can do. We can look at any creature, and with only a thought send it to nothingness. We can make a large tree a sapling once more. We can lift a boulder by wishing it be in air. Those are little things, but we can do more. Oh, much more. Not even we know how much we can do. Know only it be things unheard of as we know not how strong our wishes, made real, can be. Hawthorne sat, worried so, looking at me, and said what had to be said.

"Birch, we have lost so many. We have seen friends become prizes hung on walls. We have watched wee bunnies, new, crushed by earth movers, oh, their families covered in dirt to live never again. All that, and we have hidden, doing nothing, yet we can do what we wish with but a look, a wish in our hearts. Do you think it be time to say no to the big ones? Use our mighty wishes? They will never stop hurting forest and creatures of all kinds. They are villains, Birch. Bad creatures. Will you join me and wish them away?"

It be true. We had denied doing what we were created to, protect the forest and all life in it for too long. We had never harmed any creature, and it was our knowing that big ones be creatures too that kept us from wishing them away. We talked if there was any other way, then thought of how we had seen, just a while back, big ones who too wanted such harm to all things to stop. Those big one, though not many, saw the meaning of all life gathered, shouting to other foolish big ones, crying out forest, trees and creatures must no be harmed. For their plea, the other big ones, so daft, attacked them, killed many of them, screamed at them, used thunder sticks to stop many, then taking away any standing, locking them in cages. There was no hope big ones would know the nature of living things, even living ones of their own kind.

I looked at Hawthorne and agreed we must stop the big ones. Hawthorne looked sadder than I could imagine, and sad was I as well. Few, if any, knew the power of faeries such as we. We knew we lived since all began as we can look at something… a creature, a tree about to fall on us… and wish it away. We know not where it goes, but it does go away. Just a thought in our minds, nothing more. This is why sadness inside us must ever be a feeling, never an anger. Hawthorne could look at big ones, their boxes, earth movers, then get mad or frightened and will them away. Both of us knew our sadness was turning to anger. We knew that the big ones must stop being big, and our anger would be bigger than them.

Returning to our tree, Douglas, we sat in our hollow, knothole covered to keep our light from shining at night so creatures may sleep. Hawthorne looked at me and I saw her strife. She felt mine. The time of anger had arrived. None far from our little knothole, a box had appeared.

We had mystery running in our thoughts as new box had no paths, no way to reach it except from above. Near our own tree, a sacred place, the box appeared, no sound being made, no earth movers made it, no big ones roaming near, and it be a mystery true. It be a large one, having many holes in it, ones we get near to see big ones inside if we wished. The color of the thing was much same as color of the mountain rocks and earth around it, and only few trees, long passed, were moved aside for box to sit in their place. I thought of the mystery, thinking how little we knew of big ones. We saw all from afar, never hearing much of what they say or do when not tearing down the forest.

"Hawthorne, it be true big ones be like night without moon, dark in nature, thinking not of the many who live here. They see trees only as boxes, and no see things proper, no seeing them as living. Before we use our might, and that is something we vowed to never do unless there be choice no other, do you think it best we learn more about the new big box, the one near? We saw it has only two big ones. We can hide in bush near. Yea, it be cold time, but they may go outside where we hear them clear. I be thinking they too be living things, and they need a home, just as we. What say we go learn more about them while we still can?"

Eyes wide, a serious look that showed her wisdom as she would think on things long before doing them. She blinked, hugged me, saying it be fine idea, and right to do. Maybe they just be daft, and no know harm they do. With that, I smiled, we ate our berries, and made our plan.

When the bright ball of light came up the next day, we took to air and flew high above new box, looking for place safe to perch in tree. The box be tall, having mighty Conifer near it where much could be seen. Hawthorne pointed to Conifer tree, leading way to lush branch where big ones could no see us. The tree be full of finches and squirrels, and we told them worry not, we were wishing no attention, so be about their day as if we no be there. A wee chipmunk, new, came to cuddle with Hawthorne and she could no turn the little babe away as he was confused where his mum be. She whispered to him we would help him find his tunnel later that day, and he fell asleep with his cheeks bulging with little nuts he had stored for his journey.

When the wee thing was snug on the branch next to us, we saw a big one. We sat still and had view most perfect to watch. We were all ears and eyes, looked at each other, then to the big one.

Like Hawthorne, the big one was a lass, most pretty, looking much like a woodland nymph. I will say she looked like Hawthorne in many ways. She was little for a big one, had dark brown hair, short, and we could see her face and her smile be kind. She moved with a calm that surprised us, walking through an opening that was much like knothole on tree, had plank on it, and watched as she closed plank behind her.

She had large cup; it being filled with water. Outside her knothole, there be large dish. She put her cup next to where it was, on long log laid to be high as her waist. She looked in dish, her eyes squinted, and she looked worried. Walking to side of mountain next to big box, she was careful in picking out little rocks, studying each one, holding them once she liked them. We were confused, and I could tell Hawthorne be worried she may throw the rocks at us, but I whispered she had no looked our way, calming Hawthorne.

Little big one lass went back to dish, took each rock and placed it in dish with great care, bending to see how high or low it be, then took her large cup filled with water and poured water in dish. We saw she be pouring in only a bit to cover all rocks there about halfway. Again, she studied it, then smiled.

Once water be in dish, busy bees came flying and flew about her, but she be no afraid, seeming happy.

We watched bees go to dish, land on rocks, perched on their edge and they took long drinks of water. The lass watched, and we heard her say to all bees to be careful, and no fall in water. Hawthorne looked at me, then whispered that be wise as bees could no fly out of water once in, and with no rocks, that would be their fate. The lass went in box, then more bees flew and took drink, all delighting in water there.

Once filled such, they flew up and we were surprised as they did no go to any hive in tree. Up near top of box, in part that was no flat, slanting like the mountainside, they went in box!

I held Hawthorne by her hand as she wanted to go save them from being in box with big ones, but I could see no harm be waiting for them. In way only a faerie can do, I called to busy bee flying near us, and the furry thing came to our branch saying it be fine day. I asked why his family be flying into big box. The wee thing giggled, saying it be finest place for hive they had, ever. A place no bear or other who loved their nectar could go. They made their home in large box and be happy there. I asked didn't big ones there take their nectar, or try sending them away? He said no, never, and if silly bee be lost and find themselves where big ones ate or slept, little big one lass would take them in her hand, then hold them up to knothole that led to their hive. With that, he said he must be away, and we thanked him and watched him fly to box, going inside.

We looked at each other, and Hawthorne be amazed. The big ones weren't hurting busy bees and had welcomed them in box. Hawthorne had her serious look once more, and she said that be for bees, but that may be only because big ones thought them no threat, but what of others? It was then we saw mighty set of antlers coming through tall brush behind box. Without any fear, large buck walked to box, and there be flat ledge there, halfway up box. He bent head down near to ground, and we both jumped as he went under large ledge. Hawthorne pointed down to lush bush at side of box, and we left the little chipmunk sleeping on branch and flew down to see foolish buck's fate.

Once in bush, again we be surprised. Under ledge, in shade of it, was gentle doe with her wee fawn, resting there. The buck nuzzled doe, then fawn, then turned and left, slowly walking, eating at various grasses as the doe licked and groomed little new one. We saw little big one lass again, but this time she was inside box, looking out hole where she could see doe and fawn. She held strange cat, like none we have seen for it had long fur and be small, and both little big one and cat waved at doe, then fawn, big one smiling at them. It be clear she meant them no harm, and we could tell she had love for them. We were most confused.

It be day when wind blew clouds our way, and we knew cold white stuff, flakes, be coming soon. We watched as flakes from the sky, lovely white, began to blow about, soon covering grasses, bushes, and trees. Seeing elk be safe and happy, we flew back to tree branch. Little chipmunk be covered in white flakes, content on branch, belly and cheeks full of nuts. We smiled at birds around us, and they be flitting back and forth from wondrous thing hung on box, full of seeds they loved.

Hawthorne flew silent and unseen in tree, talking to birds and squirrels. Birds were yawning for light be leaving, dark of night creeping in.

Hawthorne flew back to branch and said all in tree thought the two big ones be kind and were no afraid of them. We talked how it may be trick, or it be that some big ones learned true meaning of life and wished to be like ones belonging in forest. Hawthorne first looked at me as if I be silly, but I could see her thinking that may be so. It be dark, and the white stuff was growing high on ground and branches, covering all trees making them white, branches drooping far from the weight of so many flakes.

As we woke the wee chipmunk, he shook all flakes off, and Hawthorne pointed to where tunnel to his home be, asking if he could find his way. He nodded, then scampered down tree trunk. Just then we heard crunching noise, and we jumped in fear. In front of box be large clearing covered deep with the white stuff. Walking to box from forest be a big one, the one other who lived in box. Chipmunk scampered down tree, saw tunnel home across clearing, and wee chipmunk started to cross his path rushing to tunnel. Gasping, Hawthorne grabbed me worried wee thing could be crushed by the big one as chipmunk be tunneling deep under white stuff, hidden from view.

We watched in terror as chipmunk made his path right in front of big one, and all happened so fast we had no way to stop little one from doom.

Hearing loud crunching of white stuff made by feet of big one heading to box, the little chipmunk did what all chipmunks do when challenged so. He stopped, stood up, head peering out of white stuff covering ground, not moving, looking at the one headed his way. Like a mighty cat or bear, he stood tall and defiant.

Hawthorne squeezed me, closed her eyes as she put her head on my shoulder to not see the wee thing crushed, crying, "Birch, tell me when it be over!"

Hearing a loud laugh then a question if the wee thing needed help, the big one stopped just in front of the defiant chipmunk, and once still, the wee thing felt safe and ran off to the entrance of tunnel and disappeared from sight. I whispered in Hawthorne's ear that all be well, to look. As she raised her head, surprised, we saw little big one lass come out of box, walking up to the other. We heard her call out to big one standing there, smiling.

"You could have carried that little chipmunk!"

The other looked kindly at her, nodding, saying the little thing needed help none, then kissed the little big one, saying he knew the little chipmunk, and proud he be and wished help none. They both looked to the mountainside where the wee thing ran off to and hugged each other. The little one told the bigger one to look at the poor trees. She said they had too much white stuff on them and needed help. We watched in wonder as they went in box, came out with simple sticks, and at first we jumped with fear as sticks did such harm to so many. But that was no what those sticks be, an no the way they used them.

Going to each tree, now looking like clouds all white and large, the big one went and shook tree trunks, and him being mighty, the white stuff started to fall off branches, and then branches moved up without heavy flakes on them. The little big one took her stick and gently touched branches to help most white flakes fall away. They both pushed up on tree trunks bent over from the heavy white coating, and we saw big ones taking care of forest around them in way that even forest creatures could no do. We had never seen things such, and Hawthorne looked at me, I looked at her, and we were confused.

Finishing helping trees most in danger, they went back to box and went in the thing. Growing bold, we took to air, Hawthorne leading me to opening that was lit bright. There, we looked inside, and the big ones were eating. We saw they were no eating any creature. They had a table of plants, berries, beans and grains and nothing other. There were no trees on fire, and no creatures heads were on walls. It was nothing like we feared. Hawthorne looked at me, motioning to go under large ledge. Flying there, we saw doe and fawn, sleepy they be, but still awake. Hawthorne went to doe, asking of big ones in the box. The doe understood her concerns and spoke in kind words.

"Hawthorne, we had run from all other big ones, and many of our kind had been taken by them for no reason other than to give them a smile. We were afraid, our little one born only after warm weather came before the cold winds now. We walked down old path from big ones who once roamed here long ago, living in peace with us, and we didn't hear the bushes ahead for hearing things is what we do best. There, before, us was the little big one. She had no stick, and she looked at us with love in her eyes. Hawthorne, I say, and no think me daft, it be she began to look like lovely fawn. A doe, like me. She invited us visit her when we wished or felt cold. We have never seen her do anything but show kindness."

Then the thing that was never to happen to us happened. I looked at the hole under ledge, and there be the little big one, her eyes wide, holding her long-haired cat, stroking its fur.

A big one saw us!

I tapped Hawthorne's arm, saying look behind her. Seeing what I saw, she took my hand and we took to air, me shivering with fear. Now all was changed for worse. Oh, big ones knew there be fairies near. We knew not what would come next, and we hid in our tree for time long, not talking of what happened. We grew hungry, and I said I would be bold and get

colorado dreamin'

us some berries. Hawthorne could only nod, knowing we could no hide longer, offering to go with me. I held me hand out to her, and we stood before the plank covering the knothole, then moved it aside.

We stood, not able to move. The little big one lass be outside our tree, leaning over to leave small basket filled with berries and nuts, and small bowl of honey. She arranged leaves to surround it, and the cat sniffed at it, making a purring noise as she picked it up, smiling at the basket, then at us, then walked away.

We know not how many big ones there are like her, but after that we were amazed as we found no more boxes on the mountain. It was just the one she and the one she was with lived in.

It was three moons later when she came to our tree. Just her, no cat, and she had a small thing in her hands, laying it on the ground in front of her. The thing was making music, most beautiful, and we knew not how such a thing could fill the air with ancient aisling, but it did.

Hawthorne and I had stopped worrying little big one would tell any of us, thinking her kind and caring of all creatures of the forest, including us.

Still, careful we be, staying in tree, but we grew bold, standing in opening looking at her, her looking at us.

It was then she spoke to us, softly, barely a whisper, saying she too was shy, and she was friend. She asked if she could visit us now and then, for she felt kindred to us, saying she came from faerie blood long ago. I was, as Hawthorne, filled with a picture of little big one being wee, like us.

As only a faerie can do, our thoughts took us to a place long ago. One blink, and we were there.

The forest was as it be when we be tikes, with no boxes or earth movers, yet there were big ones milling about. They were draped in furs and held mighty sticks, grunting, having no words that made sense to ones smart as we. Though there in mind, we not be there in body. We be free to wander the land and learn why our faerie minds took us back to land of long ago.

Elated, we loved seeing the mountain the way made, yet knowing that was no why we travelled there. Our no knowing why was soon answered for Hawthorne pointed to the big ones ahead of us, all of them looking to sky, grunting their grunts in a different way, being more a song or chant than words. We looked up to sky, and there saw what made them sing such song. We both felt the same, wanting to raise our hands and call to vision above.

It was the little big one.

Floating above us she wore a mere wisp of stardust, having wings fluttering so fast they were but blur like wings of bee. She was wondrous. Seeing she be gift, know it was true.

After long ago time, one we travelled to in vision, we faeries became timid, hiding from new cave dwellers with clubs and grunts. Before big ones crawled from bogs and mire, we faeries reveled in sky, darted about wherever we wished, delighted in being joy to all creatures, fearing none. We heard tales saying before mountains, before trees, before ones like us, there be ones who came from where all things be from. They were called by many names, but seldom seen by any. By time Hawthorne and I found each other, all heavenly faeries were but legend. A story to tell little ones, and in time that be all they were. A story.

Floating in sky, heavenly little big one was no story, and she be real. She looked at us and smiled. Without speaking to us, we heard her say to our thoughts she would meet us again one day, but until then would remember her not.

Telling us that mystery, she flew straight up into the sky becoming one with wind and clouds. As we blinked from a bright light in that long ago sky, we be back at our tree. We stood looking out knothole at her, little big one be sitting there with chipmunk from tree visit sleeping in her hand as she rubbed her nose on its fur.

Looking at her, Hawthorne was dazzled, yet confused. Being bold and true, she took me hand and led me to little big one faerie, then tilting her head up, let go me hand and flew up to sit on little big one's knee, calling me to join her. We both sat on knee and felt same as seeing her in sky long ago. She was of heaven most special, the one legend told of. Looking at her watching us, it was easy to know she heard our minds, and she looked at us with love and kindness.

"Oh, you be afraid so long. No more. Know now, that be no more. This place be my home, and yours, and for all creatures here. Nay, not for others. No big ones know way here. It be place only for ones like we. And, I be friend. I have no name, none that I know, so call me what you wish."

Our heads were full of questions and excitement. No knowing why, I could no stop myself from shouting out, "How can faerie be so big?"

Hawthorne looked at me with one of her looks, then began laughing, then we all laughed. It was an honest question any faerie would need ask. Little big one held out her hand for us to sit on, and once there, she lifted us up to be near her face.

"Birch, I be big because I be big. It no be my doing. Just how I was made. An, tell me true, what makes you so wee?"

Looking flustered, I was at loss for answer, then realized we all were laughing again, most of all the faerie who held us. She closed her eyes, then we closed our eyes and saw the very thing she saw with her eyes closed. It made us feel certain of all things.

Trees were trees, and most be big. Chipmunks be little, and scamper about. Birds fly. Fish swim. Hawks prey on little ones as that is what hawks do. There were no answers as such things no needed a question. None chose to be what they were. They were as they were made to be. Then, we saw vision of big ones crawling out of caves, then making boxes and pulling up earth and soil. We saw a big one, holding a sharp stick over another big one laying frightened on the ground, thinking hard, then smiled a terrible smile, pushing the stick with might into the one on the ground.

All our eyes opened, and she spoke of what we all saw.

"Big ones, oh, they be no like us. No happy to just be living, they think they can be whatever they wish to be. It be sad, oh, yea, sad. They decide what creature stay living, an what creature die. An like birds fly, fish swim, they be what they be. There be no changing what they be, no more than you can no be faerie. The first faeries, ones like me, could no change them. Know we could no hide from them, for they wish to take us same as they take elk, as prize. It be true I be beautiful and wondrous, so they wanted only to mate with me, an that can no be. If a big one touch me,

I be turned to dust and be no more. Me an my mate, we flew here across time, to this mountain, and it be place no big one can see. A place no big one can enter. Just for us, the creatures that roam, and yea, you two wee ones. There be no fear in this place."

Understanding all told to us, again I found myself shouting out a question, most bold, but one fair.

"Big faerie, as ya have no name, why do you live in box? Big box, like big ones?"

Her eyes glistened and she rose in the air, us in her hand, and flew so high we could see the box her and her faerie mate lived in. She circled around, and we could no see boxes near or far and she said in this place, there be none anywhere as it be true faerie home. Gently landing on the plank in the back of the box, she sat down next to a large rock where she put us to sit with her.

"You be thinking big ones figured out how to make boxes, special, to live in. Nay, long ago they saw our old home, an copy it. They no be good at making such a place, an it has taken till now to make one sweet as ours be. This no be box. It be house. A home. It be old as mountains here. Little faeries… Hawthorne, Birch. Know this. Live here with us, for there be many places, special, in house where you may live if you wish."

We all took wing, and she showed us inside the box, now knowing it be called house, a home for us if we wished. It be special place, and it be full of things from all time, since things began. Inside was her mate, a faerie large and mighty, but gentle and ever so kind. He welcomed us, saying he worried he may scare us off, being so big and all, then smiled saying he be glad that day be past.

Since then, we still have our tree and our knot hole, and we go there now and then and cuddle with no fear like once upon a time. We live in the house of the true faeries, and we love them and they love us. It took time long to understand the ways of faeries true, and of big ones, but they told us many stories that explained things we wondered about. It didn't change the nature of big ones, but it made us knowing that all need be respected, even those with no respect for us.

The big faerie told us he and the faerie lass loved the mountains, the rivers, the creatures all around us, and that it be a special place. "Sacred" is what he called it. I asked what the big ones called it. He put hand to chin, thinking, then answered.

"The big ones who love the mountains and the sacred nature of the place, they be true and wise. If they move to mountains as faeries do, they call it home. Ones who moved there for reasons other, just running about, sliding on white flakes, tearing down trees, and some taking lives of creatures or each other, an robbing land of its nature? They have a name, strange, for it. They call it Colorado."

back home again

Inspirational

I only had to look in two boxes to find what a home really means.

Having two battered old shoeboxes I've carted around most of my life but never opened, I decided to open them and explore if anything inside was worth keeping. Taped shut with brown craft tape, each had the name Thom McAn Shoes along with hand-painted notes of what was inside. One had dark red nail polish used to paint letters on the top that cautioned it was something to keep as it said, "Important." The other was a box I knew would be full of hospital records from an head injury I sustained when I was seven and kept for who-knows-what reason. It had eyebrow pencil lettering, smudged, saying, "Accident."

Like me, the two boxes had traveled to every state in the U.S. except Hawaii and had also taken detours to Mexico and Canada. Also like me they showed the wear and tear of what seemed to be a million miles on an endless ride. My boxes and I made the journey several times over while I was growing up. They were my only mementos from childhood, and I sat wondering why I kept them. There couldn't be anything sentimental in them as there was nothing in my childhood to be sentimental about.

Looking at the boxes I shook my head, sadly realizing my fondest memory growing up was from when I turned thirteen. It was a vivid image of me putting all my personal possessions, including the two boxes, in a suitcase I bought at a Salvation Army store for fifty cents. Suddenly I was reliving that day from over fifty years ago, elated being back there.

I saved up money I had earned doing assorted odd jobs and when I had fifty dollars, my goal, I bought the suitcase. Next, I went to an abandoned old house where my keepers were hiding out, filled up the suitcase with my few clothes, books, art supplies, things I had written in a spiral-bound notebook, and a letter from my mother that had her address in Chicago. Closing it, calmly telling my grandmother I was leaving, she told me I still owed her ten dollars. I didn't reply. I walked to a Greyhound bus station, bought a ticket to Chicago, and waited two hours until departure time drinking RC Cola and eating a box of Good & Plenty. I recalled thinking that day that I was good and plenty ready to go. Perhaps I was embellishing the recollection, but, why not? It was true.

It was a bittersweet memory. I was so young, and I wasn't afraid or worried to be a runaway. I had been living with people who were runaways and knew it wouldn't be an easy live on my own, but one better than staying with them.

I leaned back and recalled the look of shock on my mother's face when I knocked on her apartment door. I had never lived with her, but she had met-up with my vagabond family occasionally, and my grandmother had some way to know where she was. Most often she was living with her uncle and aunt in Chicago, a childless couple who viewed her as a surrogate daughter. They took her in, but not me. Having me when she was thirteen, I was a bad memory and a topic not discussed apparently. It never seemed to matter to me, and I accepted not being wanted. It was simply a way to deal with the hurt that I wasn't living with my mother and that her uncle and aunt hadn't wanted me either. In the battleground of emotions, I had chosen to go AWOL, getting out of the line of fire, sadness, and longing. I had found a way to cope with things being the way they were. I wasn't even sure if she was my mother. I wasn't sure about anything regarding my family.

It is still upsetting to realize I had lived with an outlaw band hiding from the law. They never talked about why we lived on the run or explained why we lived the life we did. During that time, the best I could figure the leader of the pack was my real grandmother. She was an illegal immigrant from the Ukraine. The man I considered my grandfather was not related to me as he had abandoned a wife and kids to take off with my all-too-hot grandmother just after I was born. He was a rancher turned real estate developer in post-WWII Denver where they met and some illicit dealings at the time got him thrown in jail. My grandmother took his one call and told him she had to leave or get deported. He begged her to wait a day, which she did. He busted out of jail, and I eventually learned his escape involved violence. That made things where he couldn't stay anywhere very long for fear of being sent back for a life sentence. Then, there were my two uncles. Each about ten years older than me, always saying my being born was why all of us were on the road with an escaped convict. Every day I was reminded it was all my fault.

That had hurt me at first. Being told everything horrible was my fault was pretty brutal. I didn't understand any of the reasons, and it isolated me from them all. They were all victims of my simply being born. It was put to me in a way that I was not a part of them. Just a child, of course I wanted to be part of a family and be loved. I never had that. They made me feel like I was a captor who was keeping them from happiness. I never felt close to them and the only way I felt was alone.

None of us had the same last names. My name was a distant family last name, and being so young and not knowing otherwise, I accepted people made up names, moved every few days, yelled at each other constantly, and blaming anything possible for their misery. I didn't know people lived in houses and had jobs and ate dinner at a table together. I was used to being held by my ankles by my grandfather as I went dumpster diving for food outside restaurants, grocery stores and bakeries. I thought getting groceries was going into a supermarket and telling the guy with the apron I was starving and I sure could use some of that stale bread or those rotten bananas. It's just how I was raised. I didn't know that we were different.

As I grew older, I started to figure things out. I changed, but my family didn't. I read books and learned all about societal norms. I'd sit in the back seat reading about the rest of the world, shaking my head in awe, looking at my family and wondering what was wrong with them. My only conclusion was everything was wrong. That was no life for me, and no life for them. One day it all made sense, and it was all horrible. Feelings washed over me in waves of hurt, anger, sadness and being alone. I had no way to cope with all my emotions except to say something to myself that has never left me.

How could they do all that to me?

Waiting in the bus station, none of them came to get me. I might cause a scene. Better to have me abducted by some predator than risk getting arrested. I knew that would be the case, so I wasn't worried about waiting for the bus. That was so long ago, but moments like that never go away. They shaped me. They made me everything I didn't want to be.

Reaching Chicago, asking for help with which buses to reach my mother's address, there I was. Standing on the porch, ringing her doorbell. I was so excited. Home at last!

Waiting with anticipation at my mother's door was another moment that would never go away. I had fooled myself into thinking she'd be happy to see me. I was too young to understand the truth was if she wanted to see me, she would have rescued me from the road. There I was, standing at her door, seeing she was frightened and hearing her say to me I had to go. She had married a drunk who was also a cop. She hadn't told him she had a child and was afraid to ever tell him. She didn't even cry watching me standing there, so desperate to be with her. Handing me two twenties, she told me about a Ukrainian woman not too far away who had a small basement room for rent, then turned me away and closed the door.

I found the lady, and as I was raised speaking Ukrainian, even though I was so young she rented me the apartment. It was nice to stay in one place for a while, and peaceful. I had to make money if I wanted to stay, so I went out and found odd jobs as ways to make money and did quite well. Life on the road taught me to survive and I had decided long before that when I was on my own, I was going to earn money, get a social security card, drivers license and not live the life of an outlaw hiding from society. I had been doing art and hand lettering while riding in the car. It was something I could do in such a cramped space. Looking at magazines and books, I'd copy the slick ads, write things like I read, and I became good at it. Needing to survive on my own, offering those talents to small business owners making logos and signs for them was a great way to earn money. Best of all, it was an honest, legitimate enterprise. Before long, I started my own company and was doing incredibly well and have ever since.

What I never had was a place I could ever call home. When people asked me where I was from, they thought I was joking when I said "parts unknown." It was true. I couldn't believe anything my family said, but as my grandfather met my grandmother about the time I was born, and he was in Denver I thought that much was true. I guessed, at best, I was born there or at least nearby. I grew up hearing all about the houses and office buildings he built there after the war, how my grandmother was a waitress living and working off of Colfax and Pearl when they met. Tales of adventure and romance, so I thought of Denver as kind of my home and it sounded pretty exciting. Dashing real estate developers giving everything up for a beauty from the Ukraine. Jailbreaks, hip eateries, flashy cars, ranch life stories. I heard about places my grandfather had bought land to build a home someday. On the endless car rides, he'd describe how they were incredibly beautiful places. He had hoped to build us all a glorious mountain home, and certainly would have if only he hadn't hit that prison guard too hard. Listening to the lost hopes, I dreamed one day of not being wanted in 50 states and buying a mansion up in one of the places he mentioned. Conifer… or Evergreen. Mountains and trees. Elk, bears, foxes, cats, eagles, and natural splendor. Not afraid to open the door, proud of who I was.

Shaking my head, returning to the present, I was in a glorious three-story house secluded on the most beautiful mountain imaginable in Evergreen, backing up to the Arapaho Forest. I was in the magical place I used to see far off in the distance as a child when traveling endlessly into the night. I would see tiny twinkling stars of warm light far away in the night as I squirmed in the back seat of an old beater going nowhere very cautiously to not get pulled over. Those twinkling lights were homes. Places where families lived. Where they stayed put, ate dinner, laughed, played, felt safe and loved each other. I longed for the car to drive to one, stop, then all of us run inside and stay put. A lifetime later, in a dream home, there I sat — in a twinkling light. Even though I hadn't grown up in the mountains of Evergreen, at long last I was in a twinkling light that was finally home.

Contemplating where life had led, there I was in my home office overlooking tens of thousands of ancient trees, watching birds fly and squirrels jumping limbs. It was just the two boxes, a shredder and me. I pulled the medical records out of the one box and read the prognosis from a neurologist saying due to the severity and nature of trauma to my head, it was highly unlikely I would live beyond my teens. I nodded and watched that letter — and the many notes — turn to confetti. That felt good. Another set of odds I defied.

Next, the brown craft tape crumbled from age as I tugged at the "Important" box. It had been put together soon after I was born. Taking each item out, they told the story and events before my childhood life on the road. It had my now-yellowed birth certificate showing I was born in the Frontier Motel in Cheyenne, up in Wyoming. Then, some papers from an orphanage there. As I read I learned my mother ran away when pregnant at such a young age and the Frontier Motel was where she was hiding. She panicked when I was born in the motel room bathroom, wrapped me up and put me in a garbage can behind the motel near some bungalows. A couple heard a baby crying, found me, and took me to an orphanage. It was all making sense. Why she never talked about my birth. Her shame and not being with me as my mother. In the box were letters she had from friends at that time, reacting to her explaining to them how my grandmother tracked her down, found out what happened, found the couple who rescued me and learned where I was. My grandmother was a tough woman, and she went with my mother to the orphanage, pointed a loaded gun at the nun running it, and told her to hand over the trash can baby with all my paperwork. She got me, crossed the state line and moved to Denver to hide out.

I was kidnapped from an orphanage by my own grandmother. She was more than an illegal alien, she was wanted for assault with a deadly weapon and kidnapping.

I looked at the letter and all I could think about was I hoped they took the right baby. I was also glad they hadn't told me all that when I was a child. I wouldn't have understood. It hurt to read the story, but my hurt was not for me, it was for them. How horrible. How could they do that to each other?

Then, as if watching a made-for-TV tearjerker movie, there was the saddest thing. My mother had started a "baby book" of my first sounds, laughs, eye color and all the things' mothers chronicle in the classic way. It stopped listing the details of my supposed life after only a few months after my birth. I assumed it was when they ran away, and my mother was sent to live with her uncle in Chicago. It was hard to look at, even hard to hold.

I was confused as it was an account of my first two months, and from everything I had learned from my uncles, my grandmother hadn't taken me from the orphanage until I was several months old. Old feelings of being deceived and lied to started to wash over me. It was why I had never opened the box before this day. I kept flipping through the rest of the pages, all blank, wondering what my first words really were, if I had called a nun "mama," or if I had a favorite blanket. Getting to the last pages, there was a piece of paper, folded, not expected. I took it out and it was a note hidden in the back. I opened it, and just shook my head as I read it. It was so short, but it said much. It was handwritten in the sparse Ukrainian way of saying things.

"El. I found this in Mar's things. Here is proof you want. If you send anything here, she will not get. Walter"

El was short for Elainia, my grandmother's Ukrainian name. Mar was short for Marlene, my mother. Walter was my grandmother's brother. It wasn't hard to figure it out. My grandmother was having her make a baby book in case they needed to explain I had been with them since birth. My mother had started it, then at some point before getting very far she ran away to live with her uncle and took it with her as she knew my grandmother would have filled the rest of it in. On the back of the note my grandmother had written the date, saying, "Sent by Walchuk" (his Ukrainian name), then, "He sends this, not money my father left me.

See." It was perfect. She had left the book — and the note— there for me to find. The date it was sent was when I was two years old. I looked at it and thought to myself I was truly holding a baby book from hell. All the things my grandmother intended to make me feel when I found it. Hurt. Lies. Anger. I put it back. I was no longer in the car. I was nobody's child.

My grandfather had fallen in love with my grandmother and said he would rescue her and get her out of trouble. A love story. He had a partner in his real estate development company and the partner caught him taking all the money out of the office safe. He was arrested and put in jail. My grandmother became frightened, knowing he was being questioned by the police and she decided it was best to leave. He called her with his one call, and she explained to him that she couldn't be caught. He told her no matter what, he'd be there by the next morning to take her and the kids, me included, far away and keep everyone safe. He did meet her, take us all away, and both he and my grandmother gave up everything to take care of me. All of that resulted, as my uncles tried to explain but didn't know how, because I was born.

At the bottom of the box were black and white photos of my grandmother and grandfather. He was a dashing, powerful-looking man with bulging muscles. She was a Russian Ballerina, left in the U.S. by the Russian Ballet Company as she had developed tuberculosis while touring here. The pictures show them sitting on the hood of a nice new car, looking very happy. One was of them kissing. The little handwritten notation said, "Denver, 1955." Just them. Out in an open space. He was her salvation. She was his love. He had planned to build them a home on their own mountain in Evergreen.

The box was, as it said in nail polish, important. It held the truth. Their dream of a life together in Denver where his business was booming. In

Evergreen which was a place only one with a booming business in Denver could afford. It sent waves of mixed emotions through me. I wasn't the only one in that car long ago who had a twinkling light as a dream.

After keeping it closed all my life, finally opening the box, I learned the reasons they lived like they did. Ultimately it was to be together as a family as strange as it ended up being. I realized I had grown up in a twinkling light of a different kind. I could have been aborted. I could have died in a trash can. I could have grown up in that orphanage. No. I grew up with my family.

Without knowing all the secrets, having been successful with my own business and could operate it anywhere, I talked to my wife about moving from California where she was from, where we met, and where we were living. We each decided it was time to find our forever home… our own twinkling light somewhere majestic. She asked where I thought the most wonderful place to live would be. I told her there is a place, very special, not far outside Denver. We could live in a forest, have our own little mountain, and it would be like living in a fairy tale. So, we moved to that fantasy home to fulfill a lifelong dream.

By opening the box, I learned where that dream came from. Where such a desire to live in a place that is serene, peaceful, pure fantasy and a gift of love came from. It is the place my family had once dreamed of, wanting to be there and have a home. It was the seed planted in me on those long rides through places as far from here as they could go and be together. As far from home as possible to keep all of us safe. There is a reason my wife and I ended up in this place of such beauty and serenity. It had always been home. I thought about all the twinkling lights in the mountains, nestled in the forest, and knew each held a dream of some sort that brought those people here. Up in the mountains people didn't always move there for work. There were no companies to work at or even a fast-food place anywhere near. When the snow is deep, there were no tire tracks for days. Every mountain home had a story. I hoped they were a lot nicer than mine. No matter what, I knew being here was a choice. Compared to wherever they came from, no matter what any may be running from, or running to, I guessed they'd rather be in Colorado.

It took a few twists and turns to get here, but hey, it's good to be back home again.

about the author

terry ulick

Taking roads less traveled was my way home.

Author, publisher, photographer and designer, Terry Ulick has been writing books since 1970. His most recent literary works include the *T: Demonic Investigator* Series, and *Folk Ballads Realized* series of novels published by Wherever Books.

Publisher of underground newspapers, consumer magazines, books and a glamour photographer, Terry has a career spanning 50 years of fiction, self-help, and personal empowerment books.

Colorado Dreamin' is his first collection of short fiction.

He is a native of Colorado, has never wished to live in cities, and loves the mountains that surround his home. *Colorado Dreamin'* is his tribute to the diversity of landscape, people, history, and influence of Colorado.

also available from wherever books

Recent works by Terry Ulick

T: Demonic Investigator Series:
Voice in the Night
Demons, Angels & Battle
Death Do Us Part
Angels & Demons Unleashed
Ecstasy of Surrender
The Blessing of Redemption
Six Satans
Interview With The Archangel

Also Available:

Folk Ballads Realized Series:
The Faire
Fair and Tender Maidens
Wild Mountain Thyme
3 Ravens

View and Purchase at:
www.whereverbooks.com

ROKU Channels:
Fantasy Realized
Angels on Earth
Demonic Investigator
Wherever Books

Coming Next from Wherever Books:

Dream Traveller
by Bethany Drier

CPSIA information can be obtained
at www.ICGtesting.com
Printed in the USA
BVHW010741310323
661516BV00016B/473